The Night We Stole The Mountie's Car

The Night We Stole The Mountie's Car

Max Braithwaite

McClelland and Stewart

Reprinted 1982

ISBN 0-7710-1603-4

The Canadian Publishers
McClelland and Stewart Limited
25 Hollinger Road, Toronto

Also by Max Braithwaite

The Mystery of the Muffled Man
The Valley of the Vanishing Birds
Voices of the Wild
Land, Water and People
Why Shoot the Teacher?
Never Sleep Three in a Bed
The Commodore's Barge Is Alongside

Manufactured in Canada by Webcom Limited

Contents

To Aileen

When I arrived in the town of Wannego, Saskatchewan, in the fall of 1935 I was at the pinnacle of my career as a school-teacher. By dint of hard work, perseverance, clean living, chicanery and just plain lying, I had worked myself up from being a teacher in a one-room school to the position of vice principal of a four-room continuation school. From a lowly start four years before when I received little but farm produce and promissory notes for salary I had managed to bring my earnings up to the staggering sum of $750 a year. I had arrived — at least I was well on the way.

But such is the perversity of human nature that I wasn't happy. I had, as they say in the mouthwash ads, everything. Comfortable living quarters — a suite in the hotel no less. I had a steady job with reasonable security so long as I didn't do or say anything that could possibly offend anybody at any time and didn't openly drink, smoke or swear. I had a beautiful and loving wife, I had practically no debts, no real enemies, and yet I writhed with discontent. The reason? I had this monkey on my back that would never give me a moment's rest. I wanted to be a writer.

I longed for the wit and sophistication of New York City. I yearned for a place at the round table in the Algonquin Club parrying witticisms with the likes of Robert Benchley, James Thurber, Harold Ross, Franklin Pierce Adams and the rest.

And then when I'd established myself as a writer I'd get to hell out of Saskatchewan altogether. I'd reverse the actions of my dad when he came West some forty-odd years earlier to make his fortune; I'd go East to make mine.

Actually I was committed to this plan. The year before when Aileen came as a primary teacher in the town school near my rural school and I fell in love, I'd sold myself to her on the basis that someday I'd amount to something. Not something small, but something big. "Marry me," I said as we walked along the railway track in winter with the feathery hoarfrost clinging to every blade of grass and the snow birds undulating in flight over the stubble. "Marry me and I'll take you away from all this. No more cold, drafty boarding houses. No more salt pork. No more walking everywhere we go or sitting behind a plodding horse who sheds his hair on our coats. It'll be a fine house beside a lake within driving distance of a big city where there will be plays and concerts and movie houses and sophisticated, intellectual people." I said all those things.

And I even quoted poetry. "There is a tide in the affairs of men," I intoned, "which taken at the flood leads on to fortune. Omitted, all the voyage of our life is bound in shallows and in misery. On such a full tide are we now afloat and we must take the current as it serves or lose our venture."

I believed it, too. And I still believe it. I have never been the most astute of persons or the most practical or the best able to seize an opportunity, but I knew then — without any doubt — that I had to have this girl for my wife. If I let her get away I'd lose my venture. I was absolutely sure of it.

I had no money to get married with, not a cent. My earnings in a rural school were $500 a year. I had no capital, no savings; I didn't own a thing but a few books and some badly worn clothing. I didn't even have a decent job.

I had never in my life been able to persuade anybody of anything. My attempts at selling door to door and otherwise (like everybody was doing during the depression) had convinced me that I couldn't sell icewater in hell. As for selling myself, I was never sure enough of myself or my ideas to convince anyone else that I was right.

Now, suddenly I'd become a tiger, oozing self-confidence,

conviction and aggression. I couldn't fail. I didn't want my life bound in shallows and in misery. And so I talked and persuaded. I was urbane, witty, cocky, capable of the greatest heights. I could literally climb the highest mountain, swim the deepest river. If that ain't love I don't know what the hell is.

And this momentum stayed with me. Having persuaded Aileen to marry me (how could she resist?) I had to find a job in a town where we could get a house or an apartment or something and be together. But obtaining such a job was almost as formidable a task as persuading Aileen to marry me. There were at least a hundred teachers for every job and getting into a town school was roughly the equivalent to becoming Minister of Education today.

It was early June, I remember, when I was at my parents' home in Saskatoon that I saw the ad. "Wanted, experienced male teacher for Grades 8, 9 and 10. University degree preferred. Write to Alex Williamson, Secretary Treasurer, Wannego Secondary School Board, stating age, religion, experience, salary expected, education, training and other capabilities."

I knew what that "other capabilities" meant all right. It meant that they wanted a teacher who could do everything from teaching ceramics to coaching the ladies' softball team. They'd also expect him to direct plays, teach Sunday School, lead the church choir and talk to the Knit and Stitch Club. But that was standard stuff, it didn't scare me. I was ready for anything.

I planned my campaign carefully. First of all, no written application. I knew that wouldn't be worth the ink and paper. They'd get hundreds of them. No, this big opportunity called for big action. I'd borrow my brother Hub's Buick coupe and I'd apply in person. I'd talk my way into the job.

Then I got a break. When I casually mentioned my errand to Dad, he got a quizzical look, rubbed his lean face with a long, lean, big-veined hand and said, "Wannego. I know a farmer out there. Jim Walters. Fine man, fine man. Comes from Essex County in Old Ontario." Anybody from Essex County was all right with Dad. I meant that he was probably a Tory in politics and a Methodist by religion. That made him just about perfect.

"Great!" I said. "You can give me a letter to him or something. He might know somebody on the school board."

"Why don't I go with you?" Dad offered.

I'd never thought of that. In fact I rarely thought of my dad at all. I was his sixth kid and since he'd married late in life he'd been forty-four years old when I was born. What with his financial worries and eight kids to feed and shelter and clothe, he had little time for each of us. Half the time, I felt, he didn't know where I was or what I was doing.

I admit that when I was in my teens I had little respect for my father, just as many teenagers have little respect for their parents today. I considered him a reactionary politically and a rigid man morally. I thought that he and his generation had let us down, got us into the horrible mess of the depression through neglect, stupidity, wrong values and unwillingness to change. I considered his thinking and ideas irrelevant to the "world of today."

"Well . . . yeah . . . I guess that would be okay," I said now, and then, when he looked embarrassed, I realized for the first time that my father was a very sensitive man . . . "Sure. Great. We'll go right this afternoon. Thanks a lot."

So we drove out the gravel road northeast of Saskatoon, Dad and I, and for about the only time I can remember Dad talked. He told me about when he was my age . . . twenty-three . . . in Essex County and how he'd got his first school as a teacher. "Times were very bad then, too," he said, and it struck me that in his sixty-seven years he'd been through bad times and good more than once. "Then a friend said they needed teachers in the District of Assiniboia . . . that's what this country was called then . . . and

I decided to give it a try. Jim Walters came about three years later, I guess. There's good heavy gumbo land around Wannego and he's done pretty well . . . up to now." He looked out the car window at the dry, dry fields where the grasshoppers were eating the few green strands of wheat that fought their way up through the drifted dust. "We all thought we'd strike it rich in the West," he said.

We reached Wannego, bumped over the railway track and ran along beside it past the Searle Company elevator and the Wheat Pool elevator and the United Farmers elevator, and then the station which was also the station agent's house. Across the road from the tracks was the main street of the town — a huge livery barn, a three-storey hotel, a couple of general stores, a drug store, a Chinese café, a butcher shop, a pool room, two hardware stores, a bank, and a farm implement agency, that was it. The buildings except for the bank were built of wood and the paint was peeling. There was a concrete sidewalk along in front of them and that was the only concrete sidewalk in town. Stretching back over the prairie at right angles to the main street were three other streets on which were located such essential buildings as the four churches — Anglican, United, Roman Catholic and Ukrainian Orthodox — the town hall, the curling rink, the four-room school, a lumberyard, a garage, the municipal office and the RCMP detachment.

Scattered about among these buildings, on what might be called streets although they had no sidewalks, were about forty houses ranging in size from old Bert Wronski's two-room shack to the three-storey house of McElvey, the bank manager. Some had big lots with box elder trees and neat caragana hedges and shrubs and flower gardens and fences with gates. Others were surrounded by pigweed and chickweed and the yards had no boundaries. Almost all had huge gardens where the owners hoped to grow the potatoes, carrots, turnips, beets and parsnips they'd need for the winter. Behind each house, without exception, was a backhouse although some of the homes had chemical toilets for the winter.

I stopped Hub's car in front of the general store and asked for the secretary of the school board. A sharp-faced elderly man wearing a green eyeshade told me, "That's Alex Williamson and you'll find him in the lumberyard. Just up this street." I took a deep breath and went looking for him.

Alex Williamson was a huge man who reminded me of Scattergood Baines of the *Saturday Evening Post* stories. He creaked up off his swivel chair behind the counter and said in answer to my question, "Yes, I'm him. Leave your application here. The board meeting is a week from Thursday and I'll let you know then if they hire you."

"I'd like to talk to the members of the board."

"Why?"

"Well . . . just to meet them and . . . well let them meet me. . ."

"Won't do no good. I've got over fifty applications for this job already and the ad's got three days to run. I'll let you know."

"Uh . . . who are the members of the board?"

"I told you it won't do you no good. Besides, McElvey, the bank manager, is dead against these personal applications. Give everybody a fair shake, he says."

"Is he the chairman?"

"No. Jim Walters is the chairman . . . but he don't . . .'

"Thank you very much, Mr. Williamson," I shouted. "Thank you very much!"

"Hey . . . wait . . . you didn't leave no application."

It always seems in my life that when I've needed something really bad, had to have it in fact, my guardian angel takes a hand in the proceedings. What other explanation is there for the fact that Jim Walters — the only man in town with whom I had the remotest connection — was the chairman of the board. I got a funny feeling in the pit of my gut as I ran down the steps of that lumberyard office to the car where Dad was waiting. I had, as they say in Hollywood, "lucked in."

Everybody in town knew where Jim Walters was. "That's his farm just over the tracks there on the edge of town. The big white house with the green trim and the red barn and big shelter belt all around it. You can't miss it."

Luck was with me again. Jim Walters was home. He'd just come in from the field, a tall, lean man in neat overalls. When he saw Dad his face lit up. "Warner! Well, well, well. Come in, come in. Bertha'll be glad to see you."

"Well," said Dad, "I realize it's a bad time to come calling . . . seeding time . . ."

"Grain's all in. Just got a couple of slough bottoms to do and we're finished. Come in. You're just in time for lunch."

So we went in and Bertha Walters was glad to see us and we sat down in the parlour and Jim Walters and Dad began to talk about Old Ontario. I coughed a couple of times and Dad remembered I was there and explained why we'd come.

Jim Walters beamed on me. Now I'd met a lot of school-board chairmen in my day but this was the first one that ever beamed on me. Usually they looked at me with great suspicion and resentment as if to say — "Why in hell can't you let a busy man alone?" For school-teachers were beggars then, begging for the right to work long and hard and faithfully for practically nothing. We were like whipped curs, tail between the legs, begging for scraps. But this man beamed on me.

"The secretary is Alex Williamson at the lumberyard. Leave your application . . ."

"I've been there," I cut in. "I hoped I might meet the other members of the board."

"Hmmm . . . yes . . . a bit irregular . . . but we might manage it. Tell me about yourself."

So I told him. Gad how I told him. All about my scholastic career at Nutana Collegiate in Saskatoon, my Sunday

School career at the Westminster Boy's Club, my dramatic career at the collegiate and the Saskatoon Normal School, my athletic career as coach of baseball teams. There was nothing I couldn't do. Hire me and your school, village, whole township in fact will enter into a new era of education, sport and culture.

He listened kindly. He'd heard it all before. Every teacher applying for a job told the same lies, made the same claims, promised the same wonders. We were all so desperate for jobs we'd say anything. No wonder so many of us left the profession at the first chance we got.

Many years later, after the world war that put an end to all this poverty, I found myself the chairman of a school board in the town of Streetsville, Ontario. And wouldn't you know the situation had completely reversed. Now it was the boards that begged teachers to come and work for them. Each spring at hiring time we'd head for Toronto equipped with posters, brochures and cooked-up statistics about our town. Along with dozens of other boards we'd set up shop in one of the rooms of the Normal School and throw out bait for teachers. Ironically, once again I was the pleader, the convincer. "Ours is a fast-growing community. We're building new schools all the time. We can guarantee you'll be a principal within two or three years." They yawned in my face.

To get back to Jim Walters. After I'd told him my little lies he set me up for the big one. Rubbing his leathery face with a long hand he looked at me sharply and said, "There's one thing I'm definite about. We've got some pretty fine young men in the upper grades and we want our teachers to set a good example. I absolutely would never hire a teacher who drinks. You don't drink, do you?"

Well it was a direct question, all right, and so I gave him a direct answer. Looking straight into his piercing blue eyes I thrust my chin out just a little said, "No, I've never found I had any need for alcohol." Just like that.

I glanced at Dad out of the corner of my eye and the look on his face was something to see. Here was Dad, a good Methodist who'd raised a good United Church type son, a man who never told a deliberate lie in his life, listening to his son tell the whopper of all time.

Dad knew that I drank on occasion. Couldn't help but know. There was the evening in the summer I'd been washing cans in Frank Lord's creamery where Hub was a buttermaker and after work we'd picked up a dozen beer at the liquor store and driven down to the river bank to drink them. (There were no beer parlours in Saskatchewan then.) And since we couldn't take any bottles of beer home with us we put it all home inside of us. And we were in pretty good shape. During supper we giggled a lot and sang a duet for the family, and as a culmination of foolishness I slowly and deliberately dropped the shell of my hard-boiled egg into Mother's cup of tea.

There were other times, too, so that Dad knew I was lying. I've often wondered about the mental torment that must have gone through the good Christian man. Should he blow the gaff on me and ruin my chances for the job or should he jeopardize his religion and possibly his chances of eternal salvation and keep his mouth shut? He kept his mouth shut and I'll be forever grateful to him for doing so.

Jim Walters was hooked but I still had the problem of the other two board members. "I don't know about us having a meeting right today," Walters demurred. "Might not be fair to the other applicants, you know."

Then I got cunning. "That's what Alex Williamson said. He said Mr. McElvey, the banker, would never permit it." I leaned just a bit on the word banker because there was no greater hatred existed anywhere than the hatred between farmer and banker during the Thirties in Saskatchewan. Compared to it, the feeling of Irish Catholics for their Protestant brothers is one of deep affection.

Walters bristled like a badger who sniffs a coyote. "He

said that, did he? Well, it just so happens Barry McElvey don't run this school board. He may think he runs everything else but not this. You have lunch with us and we'll drive to town and see who we can dig up."

We called first on Peter Friesen, the other member of the board. He was a young, handsome farm-implement dealer in a windbreaker, whose interest in school matters was somewhat less than nothing. "Whatever you say is okay with me, Jim." Jim was his biggest customer.

"How about a meeting this afternoon. Say just after the bank closes?"

"Sure, sure, I'm not going anywhere."

McElvey, the banker, was a different story. A rotund, cautious man in a good suit and white shirt, he looked at me with great suspicion. "Leave your application with Alex Williamson," he grunted when Jim Walters had introduced us.

"I was thinking we might have a meeting this afternoon and settle the matter," Walters suggested.

"Don't like it." McElvey rearranged some papers on his desk to indicate he was busy. Jim Walters sat down on a hard-backed chair to indicate he wasn't to be put off so easily.

"I thought . . . maybe . . . if . . ." I began.

"Know how many applications we've had for this position?" McElvey interrupted, leaning towards me, tapping his desk with a pencil.

"Uh . . . Mr. Williamson said over fifty . . ."

"Sixty-two. After today's mail that's the number. Couldn't possibly interview them all personally. Out of the question."

"I'm not so interested in any of those sixty-two as I am in this young man here," Walters said. "I'm calling a special meeting for four o'clock in the lumberyard office." He got up and I got up, but from the look on McElvey's face I knew it was going to be bad.

Dad and I walked around the town waiting for the meet-

The Night We Stole The Mountie's Car

ing and I tried to imagine what it would be like living there. It was small, but it had an air of prosperity. Right then that scattered collection of buildings represented everything I wanted out of life.

At four o'clock sharp I presented myself at the lumberyard office. They were all there, Walters, Friesen, and McElvey. Big Alex Williamson looked at me quizzically as I entered. Walters declared the meeting opened and waived the reading of the minutes of the last meeting. Then right away McElvey looked at me hard and barked, "Got a degree?"

"No. But I'm working on it . . . extramural classes . . . summer school. . ."

"Hmm . . . long haul that. How many applications have we got from degree men, Alex?"

"Twenty. Maybe twenty-five. I'm not sure."

"Well, check it for me." He was being the big executive. I could see that Walters was getting red around the neck.

"What qualifications have you got?" McElvey asked, and his tone implied that nothing else was as important.

So I went into my sincere and earnest routine again. I outlined all the things I'd done and many I hadn't. Really, when you came right down to it there was nothing I couldn't or wouldn't do for the kids and the community.

Friesen listened politely, wondering no doubt about whether Jim Walters was really going to buy that tractor or not. Walters fidgeted uncomfortably; he'd heard it all before. McElvey yawned a couple of times and glanced at his watch. I was obviously wasting his time.

And as he talked and yawned I could see my chances fading, fading. I began to sweat; I felt reckless. I almost blew it right there. That son-of-a-bitch banker had me and he knew it.

"Well, I don't really think we can hold out much hope since you haven't got a degree and we've already got. . ." He looked at Williamson.

A Lucky Young Man

"Twenty-three," the secretary filled in for him. He'd looked it up while I was talking.

"Twenty-three applications from men with B.A. degrees." He started to get out of his chair as though preparing to leave the office.

"Now just a minute, Barry," Walters stood up tall and lean and determined. "Just hold on a minute here. We had a degree man in that position before, you mind. And he was no good at all. Why he didn't even have any morals."

"I know, Jim, I know. I didn't say we should hire a degree man. But we should treat all the applicants the same."

"I'm not so sure about that. Here's a young man from a good family. He comes out here to see us. That counts for something. Besides, I know his father and that counts for more. I hate hiring anybody sight unseen."

I had hope again. "I'd be most grateful if I could get something definite today," I ventured humbly.

"Sure save a hell of a lot of time," Peter Friesen put in. "I hate the thought of reading those applications." He reached for his tobacco to roll a cigaret.

"But it's not fair to the others," McElvey repeated. "We've got to do this thing right."

Then I had to choke down an almost overpowering urge to stand up and tell them to stick their job up their keisters one after another. Who in hell did they think they were, I fumed inwardly, sitting there in self-satisfied omnipotence having the gall to tell me that I wasn't good enough for them. I could feel it coming and I didn't know if I could contain it.

Jim Walters rescued me. His Methodist stubbornness had come to the fore. He hadn't built up a big farm single-handed by letting himself be pushed around by bankers. "I don't see why we can't settle this right now. Young man . . . how would you like to wait outside while we talk this over."

So I went, and left those three to decide my future. I knew if I missed this one I'd never get as good a chance again. I hated to leave, but I had to.

Dad and I sat in Hub's Buick coupe there in front of the lumberyard while the shadows of the grain elevators lengthened and crept across the rutted road. A team of Clydes pulling a Bennett buggy clanked down the street. The gusty wind picked up papers and dirt and swirled them around while a couple of farmers talking in front of the pool hall held onto their hats. A mangy farm collie sniffed the front wheel of the Buick and lifted his leg. Somewhere the town curfew bell clanged out the fact that it was six o'clock.

I'd have taken Dad into the Chinese restaurant for a plate of their greasy food, but I didn't have any money in my pocket. That's one of the things I remember most vividly about the depression years — not having any money in your pocket, not even loose change.

We didn't talk, each of us absorbed with his own thoughts. Mine of the future; his no doubt of the past. If I could just get this job I might break out of the prison I was in. I wanted that damned job so much that my guts ached for it.

And Dad? Maybe his thoughts went back to when he was young. When he worked all day as a school-teacher and all night studying law so that he could pull himself up by his bootstraps and give his family a break. He'd done that. Through good times and bad he'd provided us with a good home and parents we could be proud of. I thought then that he was horrified at my big lie, but now I'm sure he understood it, maybe even approved of it. For he was above all a just man, and in 1935 there was little justice for the young.

Finally the door of the lumberyard office opened and the three men appeared on the steps. Jim Walters motioned to me and I went over. "Well, we've finally decided to give

A Lucky Young Man

you the job," he said. "But considering you haven't got a degree we're going to cut the offered salary by fifty dollars. Is that all right with you?"

"Yes, it is," I said. I knew that was the only way he'd been able to convince the banker.

"Well then, you might as well come in with Alex here and sign the contract. Get this thing settled for once and all."

"Thank you, that's fine."

I shook hands with the three men there in the street and Jim Walters patted me lightly on the shoulder and said, "You are a very lucky young man."

We hadn't been in Wannego long before we discovered that married people have problems. All sorts of problems.

The first one we had to face was finding a place to live. Aileen and I cased the town. There were plenty of empty houses, and God knows the rents were cheap enough. Our trouble was that we had no furniture to put in them and absolutely no prospect of getting more than the bare necessities.

That meant a furnished apartment. But there were no apartments or flats or suites in the town except for one on the ground floor of the hotel. This hotel stood on one of the corners of the main street next to the livery barn. It was a three-storey structure made of wood siding and had a distinct list to starboard. Downstairs in the high-ceilinged rotunda there was a big ornate counter, a group of scruffy leather chairs and an immense, round oak table there the fellows of the town gathered in the evenings when they weren't curling to play a card game called "smear."

Next to the rotunda and connected with it by a door was an equally high-ceilinged suite of rooms which I can only suppose must have originally been the equivalent of the bridal suite in a more pretentious establishment. There was a living room, a bedroom, and an immense walk-in closet which for some reason had small windows about eight feet from the floor that looked into the rotunda. There had been an outside door from the living room to the street originally, but that was now shut off by a flimsy corner partition.

The reason for this shutting off of the front door was that when Wannego had finally achieved the right to have a beer parlour, an annex was built to the hotel next to the suite of rooms. And for reasons of economy, the door of the suite was used for the entrance to the beer parlour. This meant that you came up three concrete steps and opened the heavy outside door into a tiny hallway. If you turned left, you were faced by the flimsy partition on the other side of which was our living room. If you turned right, you went through a door in an equally flimsy partition into the beer parlour.

When Mrs. Polonski, the Polish widow who ran the hotel, showed us the suite, as she called it, it was on a Sunday and there was nobody in the beer parlour and so there was no noise.

"What's through there?" I asked.

"Another room," she said. "There's a separate door." She was right, of course, but she didn't tell us where it led to.

In the living room there was a large bay window that looked onto the street, a table, two rickety cane-bottomed chairs, an old-time black leather couch with one end raised, and that was all.

"There's a radiator in here," Mrs. Polonski said, "but you'll need a stove, too. Of course you'll need a stove to cook on anyway. I can let you have one pail of coal a day . . . included in the rent."

Great, great, I thought. A pail of coal. Yeah. I had no idea the troubles that pail of coal was going to cause.

"What . . . what about a bathroom?" Aileen asked.

"There's an outhouse behind the hotel, and a chemical toilet in a room on the second floor that you can use in winter. You can get your water from the pump at the back."

Good, good.

Then she showed us the bedroom which had a small window looking out onto the livery barn. It also had an immense bed, which interested me very much, with a huge porcelain thundermug beneath it, a small washstand and a chair.

My next question was crucial. "How . . . how much . . ." I whispered ". . . is the rent?"

Mrs. Polonski fidgeted with her wispy hair and looked out the window. In the mid-Thirties talk about money was always embarrassing. Nobody had any. "Well," she sighed, "I'll have to have twelve dollars. That's as good as I can do."

"And that includes . . .?"

"Your heat of course and the pail of coal a day and your light. I can't let you use any electric toasters or iron, though."

We had received both a toaster and an iron for helpful relatives as wedding presents. We never even took them out of their boxes.

A sudden thought struck Aileen. "What about my washing?" she asked.

"You can do it with mine," Mrs. Polonski offered. "I have an electric washer."

It sounded like a kind offer and I suppose it was meant that way. But the "mine" meant all the washing for the hotel and for the favour of putting her few things in with them Aileen was expected to work all morning at heaving bed sheets out of water and running them through the immense creaking wringer. It would prove to be a back-wrecking job, but Aileen stuck with it.

So we agreed to take the place and counted ourselves lucky to get it. After all $12 a month for furnished rooms was just about what we could afford. At least we'd have a place of our own.

Well, we *thought* it would be a place of our own but we soon learned differently. After the wedding, which was very nice with millions of relatives from both sides and a nice reception at Bob and Amy Treleaven's place on Temperance Street in Saskatoon, Hub drove us the fifty miles or so to Wannego.

This was a Saturday night.

In the rumble-seat of the Buick was our one piece of furniture, a real cedarwood chest which had been Aileen's "hope chest." It was filled with all the sheets and embroidered pillow-cases and towels and things that women collect, as well as the dishes, silverware and other loot we'd collected as wedding gifts. These, and the contents of one suitcase and the clothes we were wearing, represented the absolute total of our joint possessions. In my pocket and Aileen's purse we had exactly $7.50, which was all the cash we'd been able to save from our last jobs after deducting wedding expenses. But we didn't have any debts and we were pretty content.

Hub and I wrestled the cedar chest up the steps and into the rotunda of the hotel where the usual Saturday night group were playing smear. Aileen opened the door to our rooms and we took the cedar chest through the door and a loud voice shouted, "What do you mean crop? I'll be a sonofabitch if I get my fuggin seed back from that field!"

We almost dropped the chest and my first thought was that Mrs. Polonski in her absent-mindedness had rented the rooms to somebody else. But from the babble of voices, raucous laughter and prolificacy of cuss words we realized that it came from the beer parlour next door. Those flimsy partitions and doors seemed, if anything, to accentuate the sound. It rose and fell, that sound from the beer parlour, like the voices from an old-time radio speaker that has just tuned in Salt Lake City. There would be a lull when the voices sank to an inaudible murmur. Then a sudden burst of profanity and laughter as somebody reached the punch line of a story or an argument developed.

"Jesus Christ," Hub exclaimed in awe. "How long has this been going on?"

"It's the first time we've heard it," I said. "I guess Saturday night is the worst."

Aileen was naturally somewhat miffed at this invasion of

our privacy, but what she heard then was nothing to what she'd hear later.

Hub looked around at our meagre rooms and sparse furniture. Besides what I've described, there was a new cook stove with the pipes stacked in cartons beside it. We'd made a five-dollar down payment on it at Beltier's store and asked him to deliver it. In some crazy way I suppose I'd expected he would also put it up. "Want me to help you put that together?" Hub asked. He looked sad.

"No . . . no . . ." I stammered. "I can't face that tonight. Besides you've done enough."

"Okay, Brother," he said. "Don't do anything I wouldn't do." And he left.

If anybody thinks I'm going to describe my wedding night they're in the wrong book.

The next morning I had to face those stove pipes. I realize with something of a start that many younger readers will never have seen a stove pipe, and many older ones will have mercifully forgotten them. Such are the wonders of modern heating and cooking. Therefore I shall try to describe as calmly and quietly as I can what stove pipes are like and how they are supposed to work.

Stove pipes are black, both in their colouring and in their souls. Their purpose, ostensibly, is to conduct smoke from the stove to the chimney. Often as not they work in reverse and conduct smoke and soot and assorted gook, including birds' nests, from the chimney into the stove and from there into the room. They are wretched things.

They are cylindrical in shape and come in sections, each section being exactly thirty inches long. Why do they come in sections? I have no idea, except perhaps because things shouldn't be too easy for people in this world. It might make them slovenly.

Each pipe has a sort of crimped edge on one end and a sort of flange on the other. The purpose of these things is

A Snook and a Snolly-goster

to make it absolutely impossible for the pipes to fit together. The only reason they ever do fit is that the average human is more stubborn than the average stove pipe and can swear louder.

There was no chimney hole in our living room, only a hole above the partition into the beer parlour, and from the number of pipe lengths that had been delivered, and from the fact that the only possible position for the stove was against the bedroom wall, I surmised that the pipes would have to extend up from the back of the stove and then stretch diagonally across the high ceiling to the hole in the partition. Well, there was nothing else for it but to begin.

Aileen was sleeping soundly when I crawled out of bed that Sunday morning and I had it in my mind to have those pipes up and a kettle boiling before she awakened. A cup of hot tea in bed, I surmised, might be just the thing for a new bride and might help to make up for the fact that we weren't going anywhere for a honeymoon.

Another point that I must clear up so that the subsequent debacle can fully be appreciated was that up until now I had never cursed much in Aileen's hearing. Not that I don't swear. On the contrary, I've always been very bad at it. But while courting her, partly because of the bewildered and euphoric state I was constantly in, and partly because I didn't dare do anything to hurt my chances, I had carefully refrained from anything worse than the odd "damn." True, on occasion I had had to leave her and go behind a rock or tree and turn the air blue, but as far as I knew she'd never heard me.

So there I was with those bloody stove pipes, trying to swear in a whisper, balance them above my head while standing on a chair and fit them together at the same time.

I was doing rather well, actually, until I needed just a little more height and without thinking put my foot up on the back of the chair and leaned on it. The noise of those tin pipes and me hitting the floor must have wakened everybody within blocks, but it had nothing on the noise that issued from my mouth as I picked myself up off the floor. I completely surpassed myself. Old Nick Casey, our erstwhile hired man who'd unwittingly been my cursing instructor when I was young, would have been proud.

When I stopped for breath and glanced towards the bedroom door there was Aileen standing there, frail and wispy, with a look of such appalling sorrow on her face that I started to swear again. "Well gawdammit to hell," I roared. "Don't just stand there. Help me, for Chrissake!"

Well that did it.

Her dear sweet boy was in reality a foul fiend. She burst into tears, retreated to the bedroom and slammed the door with a loud bang.

At times like this I'm inclined to throw things. All over the place. The record shows that I once threw a butcher knife at my brother Morley and missed him by inches. I had picked up my first length of stove pipe when there was a knock on the door leading to the rotunda. I opened it and there stood a tall, skinny kid in overalls — Mrs. Polonski's son Alvin, who stoked the fires and did chores around the hotel.

"You all right, Teacher?" he inquired. "I heard this noise . . . and . . ."

My rage subsided as it does in the presence of strangers. "It's these bloody pipes. I can't get them together."

Alvin walked over and picked up a couple of sections and fitted them together as easily as pushing a finger into a glove.

"How in hell did you do that?"

"It's these ridges along the side. Here where the pipes have a seam. You just have to make sure that they're next to each other. Like so." He picked up another length and slid them together.

"Oh."

"Where were you planning to have your smoke go?" Alvin asked.

"Why . . . into that chimney." I pointed to the hole in the partition.

"That ain't a chimney. That's just a hole. Chimney's over at the far side of the beer parlour."

"Oh."

"Tell you what. I'll help you put up these pipes if you'll help me string the other pipes across the beer parlour."

"Agreed!"

He led the way to the basement where we got two stepladders and it's surprising how easily we put up those pipes. A wire suspended from a hook in the ceiling that I hadn't noticed, perhaps because it was so high above my head, held the pipes in the centre. We were ready for our first fire.

By this time Aileen had got over the shock of my swearing and, wearing a fetching, flimsy thing I'd never seen before, came out to cook our first breakfast. I got some kindling and some paper, adjusted the dampers on the pipes, opened the draft and lit the fire. It caught and went fine.

And then for no reason I could see little curls of smoke begin rising from the surface of the stove and puffing out around the oven door. And they stunk.

Aileen retreated to the bedroom again while I set out to find Alvin whom I met on the cellar steps carrying a huge tubful of ashes. Since there were rarely any travellers in the hotel on Sunday and since the beer parlour was closed, it was the day for the general cleanup. When we got back to the apartment the place was full of a foul-smelling smoke.

"Open the window," Alvin commanded. "It's the oil on the stove. They always put it on new stoves to keep them from rusting. It'll burn off in an hour or so."

It did, too. Aileen and I ate our first breakfast in the

hotel dining room at a cost of seventy cents for the two of us. I don't know why, but in the Thirties the standard price of an ordinary full-course restaurant meal was always thirty-five cents. Very reasonable, provided you've got the thirty-five cents.

So we settled in our new home, in many ways the most all-round fascinating home we've ever had. True we had no television or radio but the entertainment from the adjoining beer parlour was far better. Once Aileen's delicate ears became attuned to the language we found the arguments, discussions, business deals, tall stories, dirty stories, schemes for revenge positively awe inspiring.

Some sessions were slower than others, but every afternoon when I staggered home just before six, after teaching all day and running up and down a soccer field refereeing a game, Aileen had some piquant bit of gossip for me.

"What's a fruit?" she asked me one afternoon.

"A what?"

"A fruit. I heard Mr. Gruff say . . ."

"Who in hell is Mr. Gruff?"

"I have no idea. I just tell them by their voices. He's the one with the deep gruff voice and the booming laugh who always pushes back his chair about four o'clock and says '. . . Jesuschrist, I gotta meet the four-fifteen' and leaves."

"Oh that must be Percy Shannon. He picks up the express from the four-fifteen train and delivers it to the stores. He owns the stable and the pool hall. Who did he call a fruit?"

"Somebody called . . . I think he said 'Chicken!' . . . could it be 'chicken dirt'?"

"Henshit. He's one of the elevator men . . ."

"Why do they call him such an awful name?"

"Because his name is Henshaw . . . naturally. Besides, the name suits him. He's a prissy little man. Probably is a fairy . . . come to think of it."

"Now *you're* doing it. I think that's an awful thing to say."

A Snook and a Snolly-goster

"How come you know 'fairy' and not 'fruit'?"

"I've got brothers, you know."

"Okay, fruit and fairy mean the same. What else is new?"

"Who's Ruby? Every time anybody mentioned her they all laugh."

"That's Ruby Sloane. Big family of them live in that shack just down the street towards the school. Her father is the honey-dipper man. You know . . . cleans out the outdoor toilets, helps in the slaughter house and does most of the other miserable jobs around town."

"Is she a rather big girl with sort of straggly hair?"

"Yeah. You've probably seen her . . ."

"I saw her from our bedroom window going into the back of the livery stable."

"That's what they were laughing about!"

"Those men? What do you mean?"

"Well . . . let's see . . . how can I put this. The livery barn faces the main street. And it's a perfectly natural place for any respectable citizen to go . . . you know . . . to see about a horse or pass the time of day with old Percy Shannon . . . except he's hardly ever there these days. Actually they don't fool anybody."

"And Ruby goes in the back door?"

"That's what I hear. She's rather simple, I'm afraid, or should we say, easily persuaded."

"That's terrible. What men?"

"Well . . . uh . . . it's only gossip, you understand . . ."

"There's no truth in it, either, I bet, or you just made it up."

"No, no," I blabbed. "Ruby's famous for miles. Has some mighty influential friends, too."

"Like who?"

"Well, a couple of years ago she became pregnant and her father was furious. He needed another mouth to feed like he needs more mice. So he called in Sergeant Stoneman to find the guilty party."

"The father, you mean? Who was it?"

"First Stoneman interviewed Ruby and she gave him a list of names . . . about twenty, they say . . . who could have been the father. When Stoneman looked at that list he almost fell over. Some of our best citizens were on it!"

"What did he do?"

"He called a little informal meeting of leading citizens. He told them he had a list of Ruby's friends . . . but he didn't show it to them. Said he didn't want to have to arrest anybody . . . of course . . . but . . ."

"But?"

"But Sloane might be persuaded to drop the charge if he . . . well . . . sort of got more work. They got the message, and now Sloane never lacks for odd jobs. Stoneman still has the list . . . just in case."

"What about the child?"

"Oh it's over there at the Sloane house somewhere. Hard to tell just which one it is."

"That's a terrible story. I bet you made it up, too."

"Yeah, yeah, I made the whole thing up." I suddenly realized that this access to the manly secrets of the town that Aileen had tumbled onto put her in a pretty hot position when it came to talking to the other women. And I'd come to realize, too, that you can never be sure what women talk about among themselves. Too bad the tape recorder hadn't been invented, or we surely could have augmented our meagre salary with blackmail.

Our second problem was the universal one that married people discover things about each other they couldn't possibly learn in courting. And some of these things are pretty awful. They lead to fights.

For instance there was no way Aileen could know that I was terribly absent-minded. Walking around as I did with a head full of ideas and plots and bits of dialogue I would — and still do — completely forget the important details of everyday living. As proof of this I cite two true stories. No more. The recital of these two is tough enough on me, and I'm not going to like myself very much by the time I have recounted them.

The first happened shortly after we arrived in Wannego. New teacher, new bride in a strange town, something had to be done about it. So the very first morning, Monday, a red-headed kid came up to the front of the room just after the class had assembled trying to hide behind the collar of his work shirt. He placed a small note on my desk, ducked an imaginary right cross and got back to his seat. Since I was nervous as hell on my first day and anxious to make a good start, I shoved the paper into my pocket and went on with the Lord's Prayer.

Actually, the reason for my nervousness was that I was never sure I'd remember all the words to the Lord's Prayer. I have a memory like that. At the damndest times everything will leave it . . . like the name of my best friend when I'm introducing him to my wife. I once forgot the name of my wife.

Anyway, the following Sunday I reached into my pocket for something, found the folded piece of paper and handed it to my wife.

"Here," I said, "a kid gave me this the other day to give it you."

She took it and read it. "A kid gave this to you when?"

"Well . . . I don't know exactly."

"Like the first day of school?"

"Could have been. What difference does it make?"

"Listen."

And this is what she read. " 'Dear Mrs. Braithwaite, Welcome to Wannego. I am having some of the girls in Saturday evening to meet you. If I don't hear from you I'll assume you can come. Looking forward to meeting you. Marjorie Hassel.' "

"Saturday evening? Holy Gawd, that was last night!"

I left the room then and went out for a long walk. What else could I do?

The next one was worse in a way. Since I was devoting most of my Sundays to writing short stories, I rarely went to church. But one Sunday in November when Aileen was slightly indisposed, I did. When I was leaving, the Reverend Overton whom I'd met once before and who had this church besides the one in the neighbouring town to look after, took his place at the door to shake hands with us all on the way out.

"How do you do, Reverend Overton," I said as I pumped his hand. And then because I thought I should say a little something more, added, "I haven't seen you for a long time."

He gave me a very odd look and drew me slightly to one side. "I've been so busy lately I haven't had time to call at your home yet. But my wife and I are coming to Wannego next Wednesday afternoon and we'd like to drop in then."

"Sure, sure, great. Aileen will be very glad."

I got home on Wednesday just before six. (I had this rule that in a new school for the first month I would arrive at school at eight each morning and not leave until almost six. People keep an eye on new teachers and first impressions stick. After that it doesn't matter when you get to school or leave.) My wife was looking puzzled. She had just got home from downtown, and something was bothering her.

"It's a funny thing," she said.

"What is?"

"Well . . . this afternoon . . . just as I got my coat and galoshes on and was going out the door, Reverend and Mrs. Overton came."

"They did?"

"I was terribly embarrassed. You see I'd made this arrangement to go to Mrs. Morrison's . . . you know . . . she's helping me with my knitting . . . and I couldn't very well not go."

A Snook and a Snolly-goster

"No."

"I explained to them. But they looked kind of funny. As though they were making a formal call or something."

"Did they say they were?"

"No. They just kind of looked it. Then he said they'd just dropped in on the chance I'd be home and not busy and for me to run along. It's strange, though, the way he looked at me."

"Well . . . you know preachers . . . pretty absent-minded."

Yes, Aileen had to make a lot of adjustments. Sometimes she fought back. In the hotel rotunda just outside our door was a huge Philco console radio. It was this radio that caused an early marital spat.

By leaving our door slightly ajar we could hear the programs. Laugh with Jack Benny and Fred Allen, shudder with *Lights Out* and dream with Cecil B. De Mille and his glamorous Hollywood stars, of which two out of three preferred Lux soap. Aileen would often listen while I'd withdraw to the bedroom, set up a desk on the washstand and try to write short short stories for *Liberty Magazine*.

But there was one radio program that I would never miss — heavyweight boxing. Joe Louis was the sensation of the heavyweights then and his short, right hook was stiffening opponents in a round or two.

I couldn't listen properly to a boxing match from our apartment. I had to be close enough to the loud speaker to hear the crunch of leather on flesh. Aileen, on the other hand, was a bit shy, as brides will be, about going out there and sitting with all those men. And she hated fights.

So came the night of *the* fight — Louis' famous fight with Max Schmeling. Harry King, the principal of the school, was another fight fan and we'd talked about the Louis' right hand, and about Hitler and the master race — we even had a little bet on. For some stupid reason he thought the German would lick Louis.

As soon as supper was over Aileen asked brightly, "Guess what I heard today."

"From the beer parlour?"

"No, from Mrs. Shirley, you know, the station agent's wife."

"Yeah . . . I know. What did she have to say?"

"Well, she's having a recital, and she wants us to come."

"A recital?"

"Yes, you know her girls take music lessons in the city every Saturday. There's a whole group of them go in. The Budreau boy plays the violin and the Siwatsky girl takes singing lessons and . . . they're all going to perform . . . and well she asked us to come."

"Okay, I guess I can sit through it for one night. Tell her we'll come."

"I already accepted. And we'll have to get ready pretty soon because it starts at eight o'clock and . . ."

"Tonight?" It was a wail of anguish.

"She apologized for not inviting us sooner, but I told her we didn't have anything to do anyway and . . ."

"Tonight's the fight!"

"The what?"

"The prize-fight! On the radio!"

"Oh that. Well, you won't mind missing it, will you?"

"Mind missing it! This is the fight of the century! Darling, I can't miss it!"

"I didn't know you were so crazy about listening to a couple of morons punching each other around."

"Listen. I haven't missed a championship heavyweight bout since I was a kid. The first one I remember was the Dempsey-Carpentier fight in Prince Albert back in 1921."

"I didn't think they had radio then."

"They didn't. But the Prince Albert Herald broadcast the blow-by-blow account out the front window of the building and we stood outside and listened to it. What a fight! The next big fight I remember was the Dempsey-Gibbons

       A Snook and a Snolly-goster

fight in Shelby, Montana, and then there was the Dempsey-Tunney fight . . . and then . . ."

"Is Dempsey the champion?"

"What? No . . . no . . . There've been half a dozen champions since then. Right now it's Jim Braddock, see . . . he won it from Max Baer . . . but it's generally conceded that he's over the hill and the next challenger will take it from him."

"Well then, why do you want to hear it? I mean . . . if he's over the hill as you say and . . ."

"Braddock isn't fighting tonight . . ."

"Oh, then it's not a championship fight." Suddenly she was an expert.

"No . . . not really. Here . . . let me explain. Joe Louis is the hottest thing to come along in years. He's got a right hand like a sledge hammer . . . and . . ."

"Is he fighting Dempsey? No . . ."

"Louis fighting Dempsey? Gad, what a fight that would be with Dempsey in his prime. Wow! No, Louis is fighting Max Schmeling . . . see . . . and the winner will fight Braddock for the championship . . . and . . . well . . . it's going to be some fight."

"And you can't miss it?"

"Gosh, honey . . . I could . . . Sure, I will. What the heck, it's only a fight . . ." There was a long pause while I struggled with my lower nature. Then, finally, I blurted out:

"No . . . I damned well can't! These things don't happen every week, you know. Tell you what . . . I'll buy you a new dress with the five bucks."

"The five bucks?"

"Yeah . . . I bet with Harry King. The sucker."

"You bet five dollars . . . five dollars on a prize-fight? How could you do such a thing?"

She was hurt, I could see that. Five dollars was about all the money we had at the end of the month after the bills had been paid.

"I can't lose," I said limply.

"I think you had better hear this fight."

"Look, Snook, it won't last long. Louis will cool this Kraut in a round or two. Then I'll come to the recital."

"I really don't care if you do or not, you snolly-goster!"

"What?"

"You call me Snook. Do you know what it means?"

"Of course I do. It's short for Snookie . . . as in 'Looky, looky, looky, here comes . . .'"

"Well, I looked it up. A snook is a fish. It is also this . . ." She placed her thumb on her nose and wiggled her four fingers.

"What!"

"Look it up. A snook is "a contemptuous gesture with thumb to nose."

"And what," I asked, "is a snolly-goster?"

"Again I quote . . . 'a clever, unscrupulous person'!"

"Ha! Well at least I'm clever, and that's more than I can say . . ."

Bang! The bedroom door almost broke from its hinges. I was alone and furious.

What happened? I went to hear the fight, of course, and she went to the recital. Actually we both had a wretched time.

That fight! I can remember it almost blow by blow. The announcer . . . I think his name was Clem McCarthy . . . was as sure as everybody else was that the Bomber would demolish the pure Aryan. He was advertising Buick cars, I remember, and for the first few rounds of the fight he'd say . . . "And Louis comes in with a left . . . all the power of a new Buick!"

But then the fight began to turn. It seemed that every time Louis threw the left he dropped his shoulder and the German was coming in over it with a straight right that landed hard on Louis' temple and hurt. Around about the fifth round this punishment had slowed down the Bomber and it looked as though he might lose. Suddenly, according to McCarthy, it was Schmeling's punches that had the power of a new Buick. As everybody knows, Schmeling knocked Louis out in the eighth, and I lost five dollars.

And then damned if Harry King didn't show up to collect. He insisted that I accompany him to a bootlegger's where, he said, I could "drown my sorrows."

I drowned them all right. Unfortunately I almost drowned myself, too, and when I got home about one in the morning Aileen was back from the recital and in bed but not asleep. She wouldn't talk to me, and I went to sleep feeling hard-done-by and completely miserable.

Worse than that, I slept in the next morning and hurried off to school without breakfast and without fetching a pail of coal.

I must explain about that coal. The weather was getting cool and that one pail of coal Mrs. Polonski allowed us had to last all day. I always fetched the coal first thing in the morning because the rotunda was empty then and to get it I had to walk across the rotunda, around the registration desk and down into the cellar. Then I'd come back by the same route, hoping that Mrs. Polonski wouldn't be there to see how much coal I had.

For I don't suppose anybody ever got as many pieces of coal in one small pail as I managed. After I'd filled it to the brim I would build up the load on top, carefully, piece by piece, until it extended right up to the handle. Then, ever so gently, I'd lift that pail and, carrying it like a basketful of eggs, climb the rickety wooden steps and creep back around the registration desk into the rotunda.

Mrs. Polonski was always there and she watched me like a hawk. She was waiting for just one piece of coal to drop onto her shiny linoleum floor and then she could tell me to carry smaller loads. She knew it and I knew it, although neither of us ever said it. One of those landlord-tenant understandings.

Well, after school that night I arrived home in a foul mood. After an interminable day of teaching, I'd put in two-and-a-half hours umpiring boys' soccer. This meant racing up and down the field chasing after kids who were as fleet as deer. They could stand in their positions and wait for the play to come to them, but I had to follow the play wherever it went. Try as I might I can't think of a sillier, more frustrating and altogether useless way for a grown man to put in his time.

By the time I got home it was already dark and I was hungry, sweaty and mad. I opened the door and there was Aileen, hungry, cold and mad. A frigid wind was blowing on the front window and when that happened nothing would keep it out. It whistled in around the rickety frame, ignoring the weather stripping completely. And since, like many landlords, Mrs. Polonski started the furnace according to the calendar rather than the temperature, the place was freezing.

"Where have you been?" Aileen demanded.

"In the livery stable with Ruby. We were having so much fun I didn't notice the time. Supper ready?"

"No."

"Why in hell not?"

"Because the fire is out and the coal pail is empty. I'd have got some coal myself but you told me never to carry that heavy a load."

"I know, I know. Hand me that damned pail."

As I steamed through the lobby I noticed that there were two sleek, well-fed men sitting there listening to the news. They were dressed in black suits and white shirts and shiny shoes and spats. From the way Joe Anderson, the bank clerk who boarded in the hotel, was squirming obsequiously, I surmised they were bank inspectors.

This made me madder than ever. For like all good red-blooded young men of the Thirties I hated banks and bankers. Somehow they were responsible for all our

A Snook and a Snolly-goster

troubles. So, when I got to the basement my anger and hunger (I'm always bitchy when hungry) and my weariness prompted me to pile even more coal on the top of my pail. I wouldn't have believed it possible.

Then with great care I manoeuvred it up the cellar stairs and into the rotunda. Looking neither to the left or the right I started towards my own door. But the evening news was still on and my attention was grabbed by the voice of the CBC announcer describing a riot of unemployed somewhere — Winnipeg probably. The police had put it down with their usual firmness, smashing a few hungry heads in the process. I stopped to listen — growing angrier by the second.

One of the bank inspectors lit a cigar, tilted himself back in his leather chair and announced smugly, "That's the way to handle the gawdamned communists. That's all they understand."

"What do you mean communists?" I shouted. "They're unemployed, that's all! They've got a right to protest!"

He turned slowly and looked at me and probably wondered why I was standing there clutching a brimming pail of coal. "Well," he said, "what do you know about it?"

"I know one hell of a lot more about it than you do," I told him. "And what's more you will, too, after the next election when the CCF takes over the banks!"

"Is that a fact? And what makes you think those rotten socialists will ever form a government in Saskatchewan? And as you probably don't know, banking is a federal matter."

He had me there, of course, just the way those fat bloody capitalists always seemed to get us. I don't know what I would have said next if the door to our apartment hadn't opened a crack and I realized that getting our fire lit superseded the need for winning an argument.

"Oh go to hell!" I yelled hotly and strode grandly towards my door. But just then my foot caught on a crack in the linoleum, my other foot slid on the newly-waxed surface, my hands flew up to preserve my balance and coal flew all over that rotunda. It's really surprising how much surface one pail of coal can cover.

There are better ways to win an argument. The bankers roared with laughter. The door to our apartment opened and when Aileen saw me she roared with laughter. Then it hit me and I sat down in the middle of the coal and held my sides.

That did it. The fighting was all over. We'd both learned the other could get mad and mean and unreasonable. It was some time before we let it happen again.

Having established myself in my job and in my home, it was now time to embark on the grand plan. I would become a writer. My first attempt was an unqualified disaster.

For a person living in Saskatchewan in the mid-Thirties to decide to become a writer is about the equivalent of a nomad Lebanese deciding he was going into the business of selling kayaks. Nobody within a thousand miles was buying stories; there were no magazines published in the area, no radio programs of any consequence originated there. The theatre consisted of Denison amateur plays staged in the local opera house.

Nevertheless I decided to become a writer.

In some ways it was the golden age of writing. The short story was king. A half dozen or more magazines from the U.S. ran short stories regularly. The *Saturday Evening Post* — let us all hold our hats over our hearts and bow to the west; *Colliers, American, Ladies Home Journal*; *Maclean's* — three to five short stories an issue and it came out twice a month; a host of women's magazines; numerous class magazines such as *Scribners, Harpers, Atlantic Monthly*, literary magazines such as *Story*, edited by Whit Burnett, and dozens of pulps — *Weird Tales, Railway Magazine, Ranch Romance*, and the confession magazines. They all bought short stories from free-lance writers.

But the best of the lot was *Liberty Magazine*, published by that flamboyant promoter Bernarr McFadden. *Liberty* came out every single week. It sold for a nickel and it carried half a dozen short stories. The champion of them all was *Liberty* Short-short. One thousand words, reading time five minutes. And for this they paid one thousand dollars.

ONE THOUSAND DOLLARS! One and a half times as much as I was earning in a whole year of teaching school. The thought of it was staggering. One thousand dollars would buy a used car, new clothing, a radio of our own, furniture — an endless list. It was like steak to a starving man. And all for one thousand words, put down one after the other to form sentences and paragraphs and tell a story with a trick ending. The trick ending, popularized earlier by O. Henry, was the whole thing. Well, I was a tricky guy.

While I had been teaching in rural schools, being an upright young man with a good Methodist background, hard-working and ambitious, I had devoted my spare time to bettering my condition by working towards my Bachelor of Arts degree. This, I was convinced, would improve my qualifications and permit me to become a principal of a four-room school where I might earn as much as $1,000 a year.

The road to the valhalla of the B.A. degree for such as I was down the thorny path of the extramural class and summer school. Which meant that every evening through the long, cold winter months I had sat huddled over enormous textbooks prescribed for Math Two or Psychology One or History whatever. By the flickering light of a coal-oil lamp I would try to decipher the tiny print and ferret out enough information to complete assignments, essays and themes which I sent to the extramural department of the University of Saskatchewan. And there some underpaid professor, as bored and weary as I, would read them and slash them to bits with his blue pencil, taking out his frustrations on them, and mail them back to me with a miserable little C-plus scrawled in the upper corner.

My weekends were likewise spent in this wretched pursuit of the elusive degree. And when spring came and I could have been out chasing butterflies or frisky farm fillies, I sat in my room with the window tight shut against the song of the frogs in the slough or the meadowlark on the fence post, and intensified my studies in preparation for the examination held in North Battleford.

And all summer long when I should have been at a lake, swimming and canoeing and angling for fish — or girls — I went to Saskatoon and daily trudged up the hot, dry, dusty streets to the University, there to sit with hundreds of other drudges in big, hollow rooms listening to big, hollow lectures and trying to keep my mind off the outdoors. I was in a rut and couldn't get out of it.

Then the summer I got married, my brother Hub, who had a public school education and was earning about four times as much money as I was, asked me a simple question. "What's the percentage of all this university crap, Fat? Where will it get you?"

"Well . . . uh . . . um . . . it will get me a degree. A Bachelor of Arts degree."

"And what good will that do you?"

Thank God for men with straightforward, practical minds who ask obvious questions. What good would it do me indeed?

I knew a man, Forbes Blackwell, who'd been teaching in a four-room school. Got to be principal, in fact (that was before the regulation came in that you had to have a degree to hold the position). He'd worked hard, hard for his degree, gave up all his spare time to the pursuit of it. Then when he finally graduated he quit teaching and took a job selling insurance. Discovered he had a phenomenal natural talent for it and in his first year he earned six times as much as he'd been earning as a school principal. I met him on the street in Saskatoon getting out of a shiny new Chevy. He'd become so successful that he was now teaching other people how to sell insurance.

Hmmm?

Well, I couldn't sell insurance or anything else. I knew that. But maybe — just maybe. Once the flame started it ran like a prairie fire through my brain. Maybe if I put all that energy and time into writing I might just — I might just. Yeah.

Besides, I wasn't a very good teacher. My four years of experience had convinced me of that. I didn't have the knack somehow. I hated telling other people what to do. That was it. And I hated criticism — either receiving or giving it — and I really didn't like mucking around in other people's lives. Live and let live was my idea, and this is certainly not the philosophy for a teacher.

So I decided to become a writer. I think what persuaded me mostly to this line of work was that I needed hardly any equipment. A typewriter and paper and you are in business. Besides, magazines that bought material were available through the mail. Wannego would have as good a connection with New York as did Toronto or Los Angeles. Stamps were cheap. Contact with the market was relatively easy. I suppose I should say that I had a great, overpowering need to "say something," to "express myself," to "make a valuable contribution to the life and thought of my time." But it would be a lie. I wanted to make dough.

Also, I knew that a writer didn't need a B.A. degree. Hemingway didn't have one, nor Faulkner, nor Steinbeck. Come to that, neither did Shakespeare. Dickens had practically no schooling at all. I realized that I'd better quit studying fast or I might ruin myself with too much education. So I gave up the whole extra-mural-summer-school thing and began the writing grind, which I soon discovered was ten times as tough. But the rewards — I hoped — would be a thousand times as great.

I discovered, though, soon after I began this great writing project that was to lift me from the dry windy cold barren prairies to the fertile warm literary fields of Toronto or New York that, although it required little in the way of physical equipment, it required one hell of a lot by way of mental equipment. You had to have some writing skill. And, alas, I had little.

I had to learn to write. Everything about it. Well, Hemingway and Callaghan, two short story writers whose work I admired, had started off as newspaper men. Since there was no newspaper in Wannego or in any other town nearby, before I went to Wannego I presented myself in the office of the Saskatoon *Star-Phoenix*.

The editor was a tall, wispy man with a big pipe. He leaned back in his squeaky office chair and gave me a very blank look. No experience. Married. "Go to your little town and your job. School teaching is a noble profession. Always wanted to be a teacher myself. Great opportunity for good. No future in the newspaper business."

"Oh," I said, "I don't intend to stay with it. Just until I learn the ropes. I'm going to write short stories and novels and plays and things like that."

"After you learn the ropes."

"Yes, you see . . . Hemingway began as a newspaper man on the Kansas City Star and . . ."

"Hemingway! Well . . . I didn't realize you were another Hemingway. That's different, of course. That's entirely different. Well, I certainly appreciate you coming to see us first. Tell you what we might do . . ." He picked up the phone and spoke briefly to somebody and then told me to go down the corridor to a door marked "Live News From The Prairies."

"But . . ."

"Many a good man got started that way. He's waiting for you."

So I went down the corridor and into the designated room where an elderly fat man, very bald, was sitting at an old desk covered with pages of writing — much of it by hand and in pencil.

He looked up at me. "Wannego, eh? We haven't got anybody in that district now. Got a typewriter?"

"Yes, a sort of old battered one."

"We pay fifty cents a column inch. You clip out what we

print of your stuff each month and send it to us. Then we pay you. Okay?"

"Yeah . . . uh . . . what will I write about?"

"News. Anything that happens. Politics . . . crime . . . meetings . . . crop conditions, that sort of thing. Accidents . . . especially accidents. Special events. News for Chrissake!"

"Yes, I see."

"Send in your stuff by mail. Unless . . . a hard news story breaks. You know, a murder or big disaster or something . . . get on the telephone and phone the stuff in. Day or night. Understand?"

"Yeah . . . you bet . . . phone it in, eh? Of course."

"Good. That's all. Good sports town, Wannego. You should do all right on Sports Day. Don't forget the bonspiels. And anything odd . . . like a two-headed sheep or a potato shaped like a rabbit . . . all that kind of stuff."

Then he added, "There's an RCMP detachment in Wannego, too. Get to know Ernest Stoneman, the sergeant in charge. Understand he's quite a guy. Knows how to handle those Ukes that are always raising hell in that area. Should be some good stuff there. He's been charged with assault by one of them . . . something to do with a fight in the street . . . broke a man's jaw, I believe. Of course we'll have a man covering the trial. Well . . . good luck."

So I became a reporter. I kept my eyes and ears open for news. I started playing smear with the boys in the lobby (high-low-jack-and-the-game) and they told me some stories, too. But they were hardly the stuff that makes acceptable newspaper copy. Actually all I learned from those sessions was that smear is a cut-throat game where your opponents gang up on you mercilessly, and that a guy on my salary can't afford to lose that many dimes.

I checked with Arnold McKay, a big bluff farmer, about the condition of the crops and he told me they were awful.

"This damned country is finished. Not enough moisture to wet a bed. Gawdamned topsoil is blowing away faster'n a fart in a windstorm. Grasshoppers eat what does come up. Listen, I'll give you a story for your newspaper. If those stupid bastards who are trying to run the government down there in Regina . . ."

Good stuff . . . but not much use to a newspaper with a strong government bias.

I talked to Ernest Stoneman, a man about six-foot-four in height and broad as a door. He was friendly and co-operative and he prefaced every single remark with, "Now mind, this isn't for publication . . .

"But these damned Ukes who live north of here are always raising hell. They fight over politics and family matters and anything else they can think of. Always fighting. Way to handle them is to clout them first and talk after. Only thing they understand."

"Why do you call them Ukes?"

"Because that's what they are. Ukes. Ukrainians."

"Well," I demurred, being all for tolerance and Canadian unity, "I . . . well . . . after all. They might not like the name."

"Now don't get me wrong," he said. "I consider them as good as anybody else. We're all Canadians . . . Ukes, Frogs, Wops, Hunkies, Kikes . . . all members of one big family."

Then he told me about the fight . . . off the record, of course.

"Nothing to it, really. Bunch of them were fighting one Saturday night on the main street in front of the post office. I sort of elbowed my way in to the middle of it and I may have hit this one guy on the jaw with my elbow."

That was his defence at the trial, too. He was acquitted.

The things that most bothered Sergeant Stoneman and the three constables that made up his detachment, though, were home-brew and suicides.

Suicides were messy. "There was this one old girl who

swallowed gopher poison, shot herself and jumped down a forty-foot well. We had a hell of a time to get her out."

The Ukrainian and Polish farmers in the district, and to some extent the French Canadians too, insisted on making their own wine and whiskey. And for some reason I've never been able to fathom, it was strictly against the law. Enforcing this foolish law took up about eighty per cent of the Mounties' time and was the source of most of the bad feeling between police and citizens.

Weddings and celebrations were the worst times. Families naturally got together for the joyous occasion and, as people will on joyous occasions, they liked to drink. Stoneman's favourite story was about the time he caught Joe Perverseff. He really liked telling this story and I suppose from a policeman's point of view it was just about perfect. To me it has always seemed sad.

Joe's daughter, who was his favourite, was also a favourite of the community. She was a rosy-cheeked blonde who sang with her brother's orchestra at dances in the town hall. She was a beautiful dancer and when the Ukrainian ethnic group staged a show of native songs and dances, she was most prominent. I can still see her with her high leather boots and full, coloured skirt, whirling and turning and bobbing, blue eyes flashing, white teeth gleaming. Lovely!

So, naturally, when she got married to Pete Magus, who had gone to the University of Saskatchewan and graduated in law, Joe felt fine. He invited all his relatives and friends within a radius of a hundred miles. He even invited the Mounties, but they didn't go.

I'll let Sergeant Stoneman take it from here:

"Every Uke in the country was there, and a lot of white people, too. I'm telling you it was the biggest whingding this district's ever seen. I knew what was going on, all right. Everybody did. Damned wedding lasted about four days and on the evening of the fourth day I drove out there, just about ten o'clock.

My Short, Unhappy Newspaper Career

"Well, you could hear them laughing and shouting and singing half a mile away. I cut the lights on the Ford and just slid into that farmyard without anybody hearing me. Then I slipped around to the back door, see.

"So help me they were having so much fun they didn't hear me come in the door. I went right into the kitchen. And there was old Joe standing in the door between the kitchen and the living room, which was packed. Talk about perfect timing. Joe had a full glass of brew in his hand and was making a toast. The point is all the rest of them could see me step up behind him, but of course Joe couldn't. He was the only one that couldn't. They just stared at me. I can still see their faces. Well, I let old Joe make his speech and just as he raised his glass to give the toast I stepped up behind him and took it out of his hand. I had him cold, evidence and all. Well you never saw such a startled look on a man's face. I'm telling you it was wonderful."

It wasn't a story I could send to the newspaper, either.

Oh I picked up a few bits here and there. Ladies' Aid meetings, baseball games. The wife of a local farmer was the sister of one of the Group of Seven and I got a nice little story from her about his boyhood. But when I added it all up at the end of September my total earnings for the month came to just under five dollars.

Then my great opportunity came. My scoop. And I blew it.

To give the full picture of this disaster I must go back to our second Saturday morning as a married couple. Aileen decided to whip up a nice little omelette for breakfast only to discover that among the raft of stuff she'd received at showers there was no egg-beater. So we had fried eggs instead and right after breakfast dressed up in our best and set out down the main street to make our first cash purchase in Wannego.

Half way down the street was the hardware store of John McAllister and we entered and found ourselves in a jungle of pots and pans, dishes, stoves, well pumps, washing machines, axes, nuts and bolts, wheelbarrows, kegs of nails . . . piled so close that there was scarcely room to move.

There was nobody in the store, just as there'd been nobody on the street. We looked around and were just about to leave when from a small, cluttered office away at the back of the store came a plump, middle-aged man with a purple face. He weaved towards us, missing the piles of hardware debris by inches and as he came within range I recognized the strong, sour-sweet smell of home-brew. He was loaded.

We learned later that John McAllister was always loaded, since he drank about a half gallon of home-brew each and every day. It was delivered by a scruffy little man to the back door of the hardware store in great secrecy. So complete was the security that nobody knew anything about it, except everybody in town.

His family knew all about it, but there was nothing they could do. The preacher knew all about it and sympathized with Mrs. McAllister who was a leading member of the Presbyterian Church. The little children playing on the street knew. Even the Mounties knew about it, but there was nothing they could do, either. It was the town's sad secret, too sad even to joke about.

For John McAllister wasn't a noisy drunk or a rowdy drunk; rather he was a courtly drunk. He was always steady on his feet, always polite, always cheerful, and he lived in the firm conviction that not a soul ever knew that he would touch a drop.

He approached us now and his purple face broke into a large smile. Little red veins like the tributaries of a river ran down the sides of his bulbous nose. His eyes were puffy and bloodshot, and the scrofulous purple skin of his cheeks swelled like a balloon with a face painted on it.

"You must be the new teacher," he said, extending a pudgy hand. "And this must be the beautiful bride."

I shook his hand and mumbled agreement and Aileen smiled in her friendly way and asked if he had an egg-beater.

"An egg-beater? Yes, yes, I'm sure I can accommodate you with one of those. But wait. First there is the matter of a wedding gift. Look about you and choose whatever you wish."

I'm sure he meant it, too. There were stoves and washing machines in there that sold for well over a hundred dollars, but I know if we'd asked for one he would have given it to us. We selected, instead, a dust mop, thanked him, bought the egg-beater and left.

I saw quite a bit of John McAllister after that. Not socially, for he never attended any of the town's functions. Didn't want to embarrass his family. One of his daughters was training for a nurse in Saskatoon while another worked in the municipal office. I'd drop into the store and talk to him about books and his early days as a pioneer in Saskatchewan. He had been prominent in local politics at one time, and had been considered for a cabinet post in the provincial government. He never said why or how the drink got to him, but he had about him the unmistakeable aura of a doomed man.

Then one Sunday morning in late October when his family was in church, John McAllister did what he always knew he must do. He put his twenty-two rifle into his Chevy sedan and drove out of town down a side road between stubble fields.

Nobody knows what he thought as he sat there in the sunlight with the curious gophers peering at him and the grasshoppers buzzing in the dry stubble and the meadow-larks flocking together for their migration flight just as they had every year since he came to this district as a boy. What we do know is that he held his little twenty-two at arm's length with the muzzle against his temple and put a slug into his weary, confused brain.

That was it. Everybody in Wannego felt that John McAllister had done a good, decent thing and they respected him for it. Nobody talked about it on the street; they just shook their heads and bit their lips. It was another evidence of the gawdamned, bloody awful way that things were.

Harry King told me about it as soon as I got to school, and then one of the senior students came in and told me I was wanted on the school phone.

It was the city editor of the Saskatoon *Star-Phoenix* and he was agitated. "Did you know that John McAllister committed suicide yesterday?"

"Yeah, it's very sad."

"I know, I know. Sad. But why in hell didn't you phone in the story as I told you to? Or wire it?"

"Well . . . uh . . ."

"Give it to me now. You must know the family pretty well. We can still make today's edition. Why did he do it, anyway? He used to be pretty prominent in Saskatchewan, you know, but I haven't heard anything about him for five or six years. What was the trouble?"

And then and there, on the hot line to my city editor with the only "hard news" story that had happened since I became a correspondent, I made a remark that must be unique in the annals of reporting. I said, "I don't think it was anybody's business but his own."

And that ended my short, unhappy newspaper career.

The highlight of my first year in Wannego was surely the great Athletic Display in the Opera House. It had everything – sex, drama, suspense, and a surprise ending that nobody could forget.

Today, when we have better education than we've ever had, everybody is a critic. Housewives, businessmen, garbage collectors, professors, sports writers – they can all tell you what's wrong with education. It costs too much; it doesn't cost enough. It's too easy on the kids; they have too much homework. Not enough physical education; too much emphasis on sports. Not enough discipline; too much conformity. Education is a hot topic in the news media. On a slack news day every editor and television producer knows he can get somebody to make a pronouncement on education. It beats pollution by a mile, or even the population explosion.

In the 1930's when everything was wrong with education nobody talked about it. Teachers were poorly trained, discontented, underpaid; school boards were made up for the most part of uneducated, sometimes even illiterate, farmers and businessmen. But nobody cared. When given a chance, speakers absent-mindedly mouthed platitudes about how our education system was "second to none" and about how we were "building this rugged land on firm foundations."

Only the teachers knew what was wrong and worried about it. But the teachers were so low in the social and economic pecking order that their voices were rarely heeded.

I considered then and still do that I was fortunate to be associated with a man with such sensible ideas on schooling as our principal, Harry King. He was a lean, hard-faced, square-jawed, dapper young man who reminded me more than anything of the movie star, George Raft. And he was neat. Neatness was in his carefully parted black hair, his pressed suit, his shined shoes, his speech and his walk. He never left so much as a paper clip on his desk top overnight, and if he found anything out of place anywhere in the school his jaw muscles would twitch and his eyes would narrow with annoyance.

He ran a neat school in every way. His idea was to cover all the prescribed work thoroughly, with the least possible bother for students and teachers. Since the best way to do this was to have a proper relationship between those two groups, he ran – to adapt a Navy term – a tight school. Absolutely no nonsense. Students came into school in an orderly and quiet manner (he was dead against having them march in, arguing that in life nobody marched into a house, for instance, or a community hall), took their seats neatly and quietly and went about their neat work. At recess and noon hour each kid was organized into a neat game (when he wasn't eating, of course) which was supervised by a teacher.

Harry King didn't pander to the kids. He didn't kowtow to them or make a patsy of himself trying to please them or interest them or motivate them or inspire them. He taught them.

He didn't take this education thing too seriously. "School," he said, "is a dull place. Teachers are dull, kids are dull. There's no use trying to make it anything else. Anyway, why should everything be fun?" He made rules and posted them on the bulletin board. Those who adhered to the rules and fitted into Harry's neat set-up were treated well and courteously and with fairness; those who didn't were kicked out.

Teaching, to Harry King, was a job. Something to do for money between the hours of nine and four. And since he believed that anything worth doing was worth doing well, he did it well. He didn't have to be dedicated to it, or make great sacrifices for it, or be inspired by it. He didn't even have to like it.

The things he liked were hunting, playing smear with the boys down town, drinking, sexing, curling, and above all, coaching the ladies' softball team. All of these things he did with enthusiasm and he had a good time doing them. He had no illusions about how much good or harm he could do the children. He considered it imperative that they acquire enough information to pass the examinations at the end of the year and pass into the next grade. Their parents, he considered, were paying for that, nothing more. And since they were paying him, he'd see to it that it was done.

Harry had been hired at Wannego because they were having a discipline problem. They'd had a principal who was a pal to all the kids. Who wouldn't assert himself, whom the kids secretly despised and walked on. They called him "Rabbit Face" behind his back. Every damned kid in that school from kindergarten up knew how to handle him. He was duck soup.

So the discipline of the school was a shambles. Big kids bullied little kids. At noon they played rugby in the halls or set up folding chairs and had hurdle races. They openly defied the teachers and expressed themselves all over the place.

The first day Harry King came to school he saw all this. He said nothing but the side of his jaw twitched a little. Then he posted his rules on the bulletin board. Four of them. He instructed each of his teachers to read these rules to his class and make sure each kid understood them. Then he waited and he didn't have long to wait. Bill McElvey, son of banker McElvey, came to school and shouted down the hall. Harry collared him and asked him to stay after school. Jim Hamell talked during class. Harry got him. By four o'clock he had four kids – from high school. They joked and smirked and wondered what would happen to them.

After school Harry talked to them, told them what damned fools they were, explained politely why rules were needed in a school, and then said that on Friday after school they would get a strapping that he guaranteed they wouldn't forget.

The kids went home and told their parents and there was hell to pay. "In eleven years of school," Mrs. Ridgeway shouted, "my Robert has never had the strap. And now in the first week . . . !" Indignation ran through the town like a runaway horse, gathering momentum with every wild stride. The telephone hummed, back yards buzzed. By four o'clock the next day a band of red-faced, thin-lipped mothers arrived at the school. They'd show him.

Harry was expecting them. They were an essential part of the program. He was in his classroom – he didn't have an office – sitting behind his neat desk. He stood up and asked them to be seated. They said they'd rather stand.

Mrs. McElvey, being the wife of a school-board member, was the self-appointed spokeswoman for the group. She stated emphatically that it was a disgrace to strap fine, up-standing boys like her son. He couldn't do it.

"All right, Mrs. McElvey," Harry said, "I won't."

"What . . . ? But . . . I thought . . ."

"And the board will have my resignation by tonight."

"But why? Why will you do that?"

"Because I can't do my job. I was hired here to teach this school, which includes keeping discipline. I've got to do it in my own way. If you people interfere, I can't do it."

"But we don't want to interfere. I mean . . . it's just . . ."

"If I came into your kitchen and told you how to prepare meals what would you do?"

Mrs. Hamell, who was plump and jolly, began to giggle. "I'd throw you out."

"Exactly. And rightly so. That's your job. You know how to do it. This is my job. I know how to do it."

Mrs. McElvey was in trouble. As wife of the school-board

member, she had to be careful. "Couldn't you give the boys a warning . . . this time . . . and if they do it again . . ."

"Not if . . . when. They'll do it again all right, only worse. And they won't accept a strapping for it, either. No, it's now or never. If you ladies don't back me up . . . and the school-board . . . I'm finished here. I'll move on."

The ladies went home and talked it over with their husbands, who to a man, said, "Keep out of it. Time somebody straightened out these smart alecks. A licking will do them good."

It seems to have done that. There was no more trouble in the school. The kids did their running and jumping and shouting outside and enjoyed it. No matter how cold it was, every kid got outside at recess and so did every teacher. Each boy and girl was on a ball team or a curling rink or a basketball team. Names of the teams were posted on the bulletin board in Harry's neat printing. And each teacher was out there to referee and supervise. The kids thought Harry King was the greatest teacher in the country, and so did their parents.

For Harry never insisted on petty rules. Those he posted on the board in the dim-lighted hall made sense, every one of them. Outside of those few rules kids could do what they liked.

And there was none of this nonsense about a teacher teaching by example. It was "Don't do what I do; do what I say," with Harry. He enjoyed a bottle of beer and he smoked and he could see no sense in the argument that because he did these things the kids would be entitled do them, too. "I also sleep with a woman every night," he said. "But I don't expect the kids to."

The three other teachers took our cue from him. Otherwise we wouldn't have lasted long. Like the students who didn't conform, if we'd come up with any "fancy" ideas we would have been replaced. On the other hand, Harry left us strictly alone. Didn't come poking his nose into our rooms to see how we were doing, didn't care what we did with our free time. All the time I was in that school we never had a teachers' meeting. Didn't need one.

Since there were twelve grades in the school and four rooms, this would figure out to three grades to a room. But because he considered the upper school work more important (this was where the product was finally prepared for market) Harry took only Grades 11 and 12. And since, as everybody knew, the primary grades were the least important, Miss Grant, a pert little brunette who was making five hundred dollars, had Grades 1, 2, 3 and 4. Larry Petrie, a soft, nervous little man much given to shaking hands (sometimes he shook hands when he met you at recess) taught Grades 5, 6 and 7.

I had Grades 8, 9 and 10 in my room and they suited me fine. Fresh from a rural school where I'd had all the grades from one to ten, with a couple of kids taking upper school correspondence work, just having three grades was like a holiday. Since I was no good at teaching languages and Harry loved them and hated English and History (not neat), I took History and English in his room and he taught French and Latin in mine. And because I knew no music, Mary Grant taught my classes to sing while I told stories to the primary kids. It worked fine.

That is, it worked fine except for all the preparation time I had to spend. The Grade 12 History course was a killer, encompassing as it did the modern history of just about every European country. By spending two hours each day on preparation, I barely managed to keep one jump ahead of my students.

There was one other member of that school staff and I guess, all things considered, he was the most interesting of the lot. This was Looie Shanks, the janitor.

School janitors and church janitors are of a special breed anyway. Through long years of fretting over footmarks on linoleum floors, they become possessive and paranoiac. To them the school or church is there for one reason and one reason only – to be kept clean. They come to hate the pupils and congregations who tramp on their floors and sit in their seats. If it weren't for all these people, they feel, keeping up the polish would be an easy and pleasant task.

Looie added another dimension to this. He was furtive. We'd catch glimpses of his short, bony frame lurking in hallways and on the stairs, and he always seemed to be disappearing around a corner. You never really got a good look at him. Like a wraith in the night, he was there and then he was gone. You were never quite sure you'd actually seen him.

When he did make a full-form appearance, he sidled up to you, his sharp, pinched face in an obsequious leer. In the manner of a tout giving you a hot tip on the second race, he'd tell you that the second toilet in the third cubicle was temporarily out of order. He never actually faced anyone nor did he ever actually say anything outright.

Besides janitoring for the school, he looked after two of the churches, the bank and the town hall. Which was strange considering that nobody really liked the man. I always figured he had something on the people in charge and was working some sort of blackmail.

And he had many things going. Late at night you'd meet him alone on the street and you'd wonder where he'd been. Any pool on the hockey game or the world series, or the one conducted when the ice would go out on the Saskatchewan River, was run by Looie Shanks. Somehow or other he was in on everything that was going on in town. But always just below the surface, like a submarine that lurks.

It was lurking Looie who really got me into trouble with the Athletic Club. Harry King cornered me in the hall one day after four and said, "I understand you are going to start an athletic club for the older boys."

"I am?"

"Isn't that what you told Jim Walters?"

"I . . . uh . . . mentioned it . . . yes . . . but . . ."

"I've been talking to some of the boys about it and they're pretty keen. In fact I've arranged a meeting in my room. They're waiting for you in there right now."

"But . . ."

"Unfortunately I've got something to do down town, but you won't need me anyway."

I knew that what he had to do downtown was a game of smear in the back room of Pop's restaurant.

So, we had the meeting.

At Nutana Collegiate I'd belonged to an athletic club that concentrated on physical exercises of the most strenuous kind: basketball, tumbling, club-swinging and boxing. I was tolerably good at the club swinging and the basketball but an absolute flop at the tumbling. In fact I had never ever managed the first and most elementary manoeuvre of the tumbler – the front roll. This is where you sprint along the gym floor to the edge of the mat, leap forward, hit the mat with your outstretched hands, tuck your head down so that you roll forward on the back of your neck and shoulders, grasp your knees in your hands and come to the position of attention with chest out, head held straight, and an unbearably smug expression on your face.

I never made it.

"Come on, Braithwaite," our drill instructor, a lean, hard, gimlet-eyed individual, would bark. "Anybody can do a front roll. Try it again."

So I would try again. The first two moves I could manage – the sprinting along the floor and diving forward, but it was the landing that did for me. I hit either on my forehead or my nose in a long sprawl.

"On your feet," the instructor would thunder. "Try it again!"

Over and over again I tried it until my nose was skinned, my forehead bruised and my neck swollen. Finally he had to accept the fact that some people can't do front rolls, but

A Night In The Opera House

he never permitted me to miss my turn. Anyway I was a good bottom man on the pyramids, and just about the best boxer in the club.

I don't know why I liked pounding people on the face with boxing gloves and getting pounded in return. Perhaps it's because there is a great deal more than that to boxing; at its best it is the ultimate in basic drama. Here you have two men face to face. Nothing counts but their skill, stamina, cunning and condition. Who you are or where you come from or how well you can persuade people that you are the best are nothing when you and the other man are alone in the ring. Nor can you depend on any team member to make up for your own mistakes or weaknesses. It is the one remaining man-to-man contest, the last fundamental confrontation left in our society. It will be a great shame if the refiners clamouring to have boxing abolished succeed in doing so.

So I organized the WSAS – Wannego School Athletic Society – and every Thursday night about a dozen senior boys and I gathered in the tiny gymnasium in the school basement to build our bodies. The oldest in the group were eighteen and, since I was only twenty-three, there wasn't much difference between us. I showed them how to swing clubs and told them how to tumble – most of them got the front roll right off – and taught them how to box. And that was where I made a mistake.

Athletic young men learn rapidly. The first time I put on the gloves with Johnny Gar I made a fool of him, dancing around nimbly and flicking long left jabs against his nose. But he was a determined fellow, of about my own size, and the next time we went to it things didn't go so well. Whereas I didn't change at all, his skill and enthusiasm for the sport increased weekly. Finally about the fifth week we put on the gloves and early in the first round he straightened me up with a hard left hook which almost sat me on the seat of my blue and white shorts. A little later I beat him to the punch with a right cross squarely on the eye. Then we were at it as hard as we could go. Luckily the match was restricted to three rounds, but even at that we were both pouring sweat at the end. And the next day both teacher and student showed up in English class with a lovely black eye. After that I refereed.

Harry King became pretty enthusiastic about that Athletic Club. It fit nicely into his philosophy of a healthy mind in a healthy body. Besides, he saw in it a way to advertise the school and indirectly himself. So he suggested that on the evening of Parents' Night, instead of the usual recitations and songs by students, we'd go all out and stage an athletic demonstration in the town hall.

"What kind of a demonstration?" I asked.

"Well, you know — club swinging, tumbling, pyramid building, maybe even boxing. I think it would go over big."

"It would take a lot of practice. The farm kids can't stay after school. Have to get home and do the chores."

"Take school time. Recess . . . noon hours. We might even manage some time off from classes."

"But . . ."

"Go ahead and arrange it. You've got a whole month to work on it. I'm leaving the whole thing up to you. I'm sure you'll do a good job."

Of all the phrases in the world, the most insidious is that one about being sure somebody will do a good job. What he really meant, of course, was that I'd damned well better do a good job or else.

So we began getting ready for the big Athletic Night. Art classes were put to work making posters of kids floating through the air like men on the flying trapeze. Music classes whomped up some songs for the occasion. Mothers were put to work designing special costumes. It became the talk of the town.

Everybody was tremendously enthusiastic about the project except for about twenty people — the twenty boys who made up my athletic club – and me. They didn't like it at all. I didn't like it at all.

But we practised as best we could. The program would consist of some club swinging, some tumbling, some boxing, and as a grand finale the pyramid building. Some of the kids were already pretty good at turning cartwheels, and Pete Walensky who was wiry and tough was learning to do handsprings. He'd got so he could do them by placing only one hand on the mat and was working at doing them without the use of hands at all – a sort of front flip.

The pyramids were simple enough. Tom Barker, the lightest kid in the club, was heaved up onto the shoulders of Johnny Gar. And then two other kids put one foot on each of Johnny's knees and stretched the other leg away out while holding his hands, and two more did handstands beside them. The boys looked very good doing this in their navy blue shorts with the white stripe and their white shirts.

The clincher was the big pyramid that included every member of the club. It was simple, really, but spectacular. The six biggest boys got down on their hands and knees in a row. The next five kneeled on top of them. Then four, three, two and one to make a pyramid of kneeling boys. It was all done very smartly, the boys dashing out and standing at attention to little blasts of my whistle, and then climbing up and taking their places. At the end they all smiled at the audience and stretched out stiff and the pyramid collapsed. It worked just great so long as no kid kept his knees bent and jabbed them into the kidneys of the boy below.

I was nervous about that last pyramid. There were inherent in its structure too many possibilities for trouble.

So we practised in the halls at noon hour and recess and as the day drew near we took time off from school. The boys got pretty good at snapping around at my whistled signals.

The dress rehearsal was in the Opera House.

The Wannego Opera House was really the upstairs of

the municipal offices and the jail. This made it handy for the Mounties as they never had far to take an obstreperous drunk arrested at a dance. Since Wannego had once been a prosperious town, the town hall was a little better than most. Instead of a big pot-bellied stove near the door, there was a furnace in the basement and a furnace room. The stairs from the basement came up beside the stage and the open part of the basement was used by the cast as a dressing room.

"Tell them kids to keep the hell outa the furnace room," Looie Shanks warned when he heard of the arrangements. "Don't want none of them fooling around in there." To make sure of this he screwed a hasp on the door and put a huge padlock in it.

When Looie let us into the Opera House on Thursday afternoon, the place had that faint sour smell of a room that is accustomed to housing hundreds of sweaty bodies. There was another smell, too, that I couldn't quite place but Looie opened the windows and it went away.

Then I discovered something about my performers that I'd overlooked. As soon as they got on the stage they were petrified with fright.

Back in the school in familiar surroundings they had been fine. Going through their routines with good spirits and laughter. Kidding each other and playing little tricks the way athletes do. But as soon they got into their gym suits and up on that stage they froze with terror. All the suppleness and grace were gone. They became wooden and awkward, tripped over each other, and when the big pyramid collapsed the hall reverberated with the howls of pain from bruised kidneys. Nobody did anything right.

So we stayed there long into the night. Parents phoned that the chores weren't being done. Little sisters or brothers who needed a ride home in the buggy hung around the hall and wept quietly. Irate fathers came in and demanded to know what the hell was going on here anyway.

Finally I got them back into some semblance of a gymnastic troupe and sent them home with instructions to forget all about the show until the next night.

Friday night came and the hall began to fill up. The farm community and the town community were there in full force. There was to be a lunch and a big dance following the speeches and the athletic display. A big night.

We had made our arrangements with the greatest care, but there was one fatal flaw. I can see it now so clearly, but at the time everybody overlooked it. There was no supervision of the boys down in their dressing room.

Harry King, as chairman of the evening, was required to sit close to the stage to make a speech and introduce Jim Walters as chairman.

As the director of the athletic display I had to take up my place in the front row with my whistle ready to give my signals. Larry Petrie, the other male teacher, had conveniently left town for the weekend. So there was nobody down there in the dressing room with the boys, and that would seem to be safe enough if it hadn't been for Looie.

Everything went fine for a while. When I gave my first little tweet on the whistle, six junior boys carrying Indian clubs marched smartly onto the stage. Another tweet and they stopped. Another and they turned smartly to the right. Miss Grant began to play the piano and the boys began to swing to the rhythm. Another tweet and they turned sharply left. Another and they marched off. Applause.

Four more boys dashed onto the stage and laid out the mats for tumbling and again everything went fine. Front rolls, over one kneeling figure, then over two, then over three. Then – can he make it? – over four. More applause.

Now it was time for the senior students to strut their stuff. I tweeted the whistle and nothing happened. Another tweet, still nothing. Another louder and longer tweet and Johnny Gar dashed out onto the stage, took up his position and grinned happily at the audience.

There was something wrong with his appearance that at first I couldn't quite make out – something a little off. Then I realized it was his navy blue gym shorts. They were too tight at the front and not tight enough at the back. He had them on backwards. There was something else about him, too, that I couldn't quite place. A sort of reckless abandonment – an unsureness about his movements.

I figured it out pretty quickly when Pete Walensky ran onto the stage. Well, actually it was more of a stagger than a run. He was followed by Bill McElvey who also seemed a bit uncertain. The two of them took up their places beside Johnny, who as prescribed bent his knees slightly to receive their feet. But they didn't quite make it. The feet slipped off the knees and the three of them collapsed on the mat, giggling and snorting.

I tweeted with vigour but to no avail. By this time the others had come onto the stage and they were equally uncertain of themselves. Valiantly the five of them tried to build that pyramid and hopelessly they floundered on the mats. Then I realized what was wrong. The whole lot of them were stoned, stewed to the gills, polluted, miraculously and happily drunk.

There was a stunned silence from the audience at first, and then a titter, then a guffaw and then a roar. This only increased the eagerness of my gymnasts to entertain. They cavorted like fools about the stage, laughing and yipping and improvising new and better pyramids. Finally somebody thought of pulling the curtain and the show was over.

It didn't take long to find out what had happened. For the better part of a year Looie Shanks had been making home-brew in the nice warm furnace room of the Opera House. He had a fine still in there and a good batch of brew was just maturing on the day of our show. The kids had smelled it, pried off his hasp and helped themselves. First little sips and then, after they'd become used to the fiery potion, whole tin cupfuls.

A Night In The Opera House

Actually, I think that on the whole the booze improved the show, at least from the audience's point of view. Harry King and the school board didn't think so much of it.

Of course there was a great deal of fuss about the whole thing. Jim Walters was for calling in the Mounties and having Looie thrown in jail. But somehow this didn't happen. Looie removed his still in a hurry and nothing more was said about it.

And the Athletic Club? Well, it sort of petered out after that. The kids quit coming to the meetings and their parents didn't force the issue. Somehow, although I can't see why, I tended to be blamed for the whole mess. Harry was most understanding, told me not to worry too much about it. These things happen. There was some talk of organizing a mouth-organ band for the older boys, but I rather discouraged that.

The post office in Wannego was at once my hope and my despair. Through the post office I could reach out to any place in the world. Just write the name and address on the envelope, stick on the required stamps, drop it through that slot in the front of the counter at the post office and a host of eager, busy hands would see to it that the missive reached its destination.

Mr. Harold Ross,
Editor, *New Yorker*,
25 West 43rd Street,
New York, N.Y.

Within the week my story would be on the desk of Mr. Ross or one of his assistants. There it was. Something to be reckoned with. Somebody had to to something with it, even if just take it out of one envelope and put it in the return envelope I'd provided. It was a fascinating thought.

It was almost as though I were on speaking terms with the editors.

"Hello, Harold."

"Hello, Max."

"How are things?"

"Pretty good. Read your last piece. Good work . . . just the sort of thing for the *New Yorker*. I'd like you to have lunch with me at the Algonquin soon."

The first short story I attempted was one thousand words for *Liberty*. And with every word I set to paper I thought of that One Thousand Dollars that I would get for it. In fact, I thought more about the money than I did about the story. Actually I should have been writing a story about a man who suddenly found himself in possession of One Thousand Dollars.

I remember the plot of that story in detail. There were these two crooks who had robbed a Saskatoon bank of a bundle and were heading north in their speedy V-8 automobile to the relative safety of the hinterland.

It was the perfect crime. In fact I probably titled it "The Perfect Crime." Every loophole had been plugged, every contingency thought of. They'd covered their trail completely. Nothing could possibly go wrong. And as they sped north, jubilant at their cleverness, I tried out all the thug and gangster dialogue that was kicking around in my mind from seeing dozens of gangster movies. There's no doubt that my two thugs bore a strong resemblance to George Raft and Edward G. Robinson.

All went well until they came to the new bridge that crosses the Saskatchewan River south of Radisson. They'd no sooner driven onto the bridge than they saw a group of people at the other end and among those people were three Mounties, red coats gleaming in the sun. One of the Mounties stepped out and held up a gloved hand for them to stop. What to do? Too late to turn back. Make a run for it. Shoot it out. So with guns blazing they roared through.

Well, of course the Mounties gave chase in their own V-8, and the chase ended with the thugs' car hitting the ditch and both the villains dead. Then the Mountie, shaking his head, remarked, "And all we wanted was to get their names as the one thousandth car to cross the bridge."

Sound familiar? Of course it does. Variations of that plot have been used hundreds of times and will be used hundreds of times more. I thought it was new and original because it was new and original to me. I had actually thought it up, not borrowed it. And this is the greatest pitfall for the beginning writer. Naturally the first ideas and plots that come to his mind are the same ones that have come to the minds of writers since printing was invented. Young writers are still doing it, except that now that many more of the plots have already been used. There is nothing new under the sun.

I wrote this story out with great care. Re-wrote and polished it. Typed and re-typed it. Finally I had it perfect. Not one single typing error. Spacing – exactly one-and-one-quarter inch margin on both sides. Name and address in upper right-hand corner of the title page. Not a blemish or a blot on any of the five pages.

Then the self-addressed envelope. I'd contacted Puss Ellingson, with whom I'd gone to high school and who was then in Seattle working as a commercial artist, and he sent me American stamps for the return envelope. Then the whole thing went into a bigger envelope. My wife and I each put our good-luck sign on it and I trundled off down to the post office.

The post office, when we first went to Wannego, was in the general store of Nathan R. Smith, a short, dapper, greying man who had come from Ontario as a young man and was trying to make enough money to get back. There were three main factions represented in Wannego and the surrounding farm community – the Old Ontario, United Church group of which Smith was the leader; the French Canadians led by old Orland Beltier, a small nervous man who ran the principal hardware store, and the Ukrainians whose most influential member was Peter Nikoluk who ran the other general store half way down the block. Of the three groups, the Anglo-Saxons were in the minority.

For this reason, Smith and his group looked upon themselves rather like Pukka Sahibs in India. It was their duty to uphold the principles and mores of the white man in this savage land. They mustn't ever allow themselves to become contaminated by association with the "lesser breeds."

So it happened that Smith never spoke to the French

Canadians or Ukrainians who were his fellow townspeople and indeed his neighbours. It was something to see him meet with Orland Beltier on the main street at noon, for instance. Neither looked at the other. There was always something on the road to engage their attention, or somebody across the street to whom they could shout a greeting. To each, the other was a non-person.

This lack of communication presented special problems as Orland's son, Danny, had the contract for carrying mail between the railway depot and the post office. This contract was awarded separately, I suppose, so that the government could spread the cash and paying jobs around as much as possible. The government, then as now, was scrupulously careful to let no hint of political patronage enter into the awarding of jobs.

So great was Smith's dislike for Danny Beltier that not only would he not speak to him but he wouldn't even mention his name. So when the townspeople were in his store waiting for the mail, Smith would mutter darkly, "*He* hasn't show up with it yet!" as though "he" was part of a diabolical plot to keep the mail from its rightful owners. Or he'd mumble, "Don't know what's happened to *him* now," suggesting clearly that *he* was either drunk somewhere or off in the livery barn with Ruby.

When Danny did arrive with the mail and plodded through the store speaking pleasantly – in French – to all his friends and pointedly ignoring the rest, he'd plunk the heavy bags down as far from the door of Smith's cubbyhole as was allowed by his contract and clump out of the store again. Smith would go very red in the face, kick the mail bags into the "post office" and start sorting. The ritual never varied.

The situation was compounded by the religious and political factors. The French Canadians were Roman Catholic which, in the eyes of an Orangeman like Smith, made them first cousins to the devil. Also they voted Liberal to a man and, since there was a Liberal government in both Saskatchewan and Ottawa, Smith was convinced they received more than their fair share of political goodies. The Ukrainians, who had their own Orthodox Church, also supported the Liberal Party, Smith believed, and shared in a lesser extent in the political patronage. This left Smith and his small group fighting the good fight alone.

Smith's house on the edge of town stood out among the other shabby houses of the street like a flower in an ash pile. Large and white and always freshly painted, with glassed-in verandas, it was surrounded by about two acres of green lawns enclosed by a picket fence. The lilac, rose, forsythia and other shrubs were always neatly trimmed, the grass neatly mowed. His well, the deepest in the district, provided ample water for watering lawns even through the worst years of the drought. As nearly as possible, Smith had created on the bleak and dust-ridden prairie, a bit of the green and grace of southern Ontario.

When I took my envelope into Smith's store after school on Monday the place was empty. The groceries were at the front of the store, then the drygoods, and at the very back the tiny wicket of the post office. "You'd think the old bugger would at least put it at the front of the store," Danny Beltier complained. "But not him. He thinks he might make a sale if you have to walk past all those shirts and piles of underwear to get to the post office."

Smith was busy somewhere in the back warehouse when I opened the door of his store, but the tinkle of the little bell at the top of it warned him of a customer. He came out, peered at me over his glasses, grimaced a greeting. I had my envelope under my arm and I didn't quite know how to present it. After all, nobody else in town sent manuscripts to *Liberty Magazine*. I sort of eased it up onto the counter in front of his wicket and, half-turning, became very interested in the pile of trousers on a table. Smith took the envelope, read it, looked at me and growled, "What's this?"

Somehow his cold eyes, wrinkled forehead and forbidding mien reminded me of every teacher, preacher, Sunday School superintendent, parent who had ever stared at me for doing something wrong. I couldn't help myself, I felt guilty. Instead of saying, "None of your damned business, you hack civil servant," I fumbled and mumbled and finally blurted out . . . "Uh . . . a story."

"A story? What kind of a story?"

"Uh . . . just a fiction story."

"Aha. About the people around here?"

At last I came to my senses. "Look . . . it's just a story that I'm sending to an editor. Will you please weigh it and tell me how much it is."

Well, he had to do that. So he did. But after that each time I mailed out a story he looked at me as though I were sending secret documents to the Kremlin. Peered at the envelope, weighed it in his hand as though testing for explosives, and let me know clearly by his scowls and grunts that there in Wannego they didn't take kindly to people who carried on in such a crazy way.

Getting the story back was much easier. The train arrived at Wannego at four-fifteen in the afternoon. By the time Danny Beltier delivered the mail and Smith got it sorted into its little boxes, it was five o'clock. The school kids who lived in the country usually waited to take the mail home with them, hanging around the poolroom or the drug store. At mail time they, along with whatever adults were downtown, converged on Smith's store and waited in groups, talking in hushed tones as befitted the establishment of so eminent a man.

I gave the editor of *Liberty* two weeks in which to receive my manuscript, read it, approve it and mail me the cheque.

After that I waited in the store with a feeling in my midsection as though my guts were gone. I watched those mail bags being brought in and listened while the mail was sorted behind the closed wicket. When the wicket opened I approached it tentatively, almost afraid to get my mail. When I did get it I'd forgotten about the self-addressed envelope bit and didn't recognize my own typing. Who, I pondered, could be sending me a brown envelope from New York? Then I remembered.

My story had come back, all right, looking as fresh and clean as when I'd posted it. And there attached to it was a small white slip with the big word "SORRY" printed on it, followed by, "We did not find this story suitable for our magazine. This does not imply that it hasn't merit. Please try us again. The editors."

That is a rejection slip. Some magazine publishers tried to dress them up a bit more; others were even more curt. Either way they informed me that I hadn't made it. My brain child had been rejected, scorned, refused, declined, ejected. They didn't want it. My first reaction was despair, my second anger, and the third determination – or stubbornness, whichever you prefer. I was to collect enough of those slips to paper a room before I ever sold a story.

After trying a few more stories for *Liberty* and having them rejected, I got the idea that perhaps I should try to learn something about the craft of writing. So off I went to the Saskatoon library for books. "The Art of the Short Story" – as a rough guess I'd say that one million four hundred and eighty-four books have been written on this subject. And none of them will write a story for you.

I bought a copy of *Roget's Thesaurus* to help me with words. Fowler's *Modern English Usage* was a must for all writers, they said. So I got that. Then I subscribed to a magazine called *Writers' Digest*, which was full of tips and advertisements for more books and the names of "agents" who would read your manuscripts for a fee and help you become a writer fast. I didn't have money for a fee so I never discovered if it really worked.

Then I learned two things about myself: first, I was a writer, and second, I couldn't write. That sounds contradictory, I know, but it really isn't. A writer, I'm convinced, is a certain type of person. He's been described as "a watcher and a listener." Bernard Shaw said something about a writer seeing the world through different eyes. A writer is a person who pays attention, who ponders, who considers, who assesses. Nothing really escapes his notice. He wonders why. Why is that woman doing that? How did she get that way anyway? What would happen if she were to do this instead of that? A person is born with this faculty. It is part of his nature.

But this doesn't mean he will be a successful writer. There are people who have a natural aptitude for doctoring, for instance, or judging. But unless they put in years of training to learn how to do it they'll never become doctors or judges.

So it is with writing. The techniques of the craft must be learned. The use of words, sentences, paragraphs. Selection – what to put in and what to leave out. Form, style, suspense, and all those things that make a reader want to keep on turning pages to find out what comes next. These must be learned.

I had little natural skill at this. I hadn't written stories for the kiddies' section of newspapers when I was a boy. I'd been too busy playing hockey and delivering the papers. I was no great whiz on the Nutana Collegiate paper, *The Saltshaker*. Although I was on the staff, the editor complained he could never get anything out of me. I wrote one excruciatingly funny story about tennis but the printer couldn't read my handwriting and so it never got into the paper.

So I had to learn. And I learned writing the way I'd learned practically everything else in my life. By doing it. Trial and error. Outside of school, I've had no formal instruction in anything.

I learned to swim by getting in the water and swimming, by figuring out the best way to do it – for me. And that was the side stroke. Now you'll never win an Olympic gold medal doing the good old side-stroke. But I knew I was never going to win an Olympic medal or any kind of a race with the Australian crawl, either, even suppose I practised it twenty-four hours a day. So the side-stroke is adequate. It gets me there and permits me to have a lot of fun in the water. But I sure had to work at learning the side-stroke.

The same thing happened with learning to skate. I didn't come by it easily. I had to learn it. My ankles were like rubber and I developed callouses on them from ankle-walking. And callouses on my rump, too, from sitting down on the hard ice. But I kept at it, doggedly and patiently, and finally I could skate – not well enough to win a gold medal but good enough to have a lot of fun.

It was the same with learning to dive and ski and drive a car. I actually learned to drive by stealing Dad's old Overland which was parked in the back yard on MacPherson Avenue in Saskatoon when I was in Grade 10. It was parked there because all the seat cushions had been stolen from it when Dad left it by the side of the road out near Warman. While they were waiting for an insurance adjustment, the car just sat in the back yard.

So one Saturday I got fooling around, rigged up a box for a seat and then started experimenting with old keys in the ignition lock. They must have made them less tamper-proof than they do now because I soon found one that would fit. Like every kid, I'd watched Dad and my older brothers shift gears enough so I knew how to do that. I backed the car out of the yard and drove out onto Tenth Street and I was away. I did this until I learned how to drive. No teacher, no book of instructions, just trial and error.

And trial and error is how I learned to write. People ask me today if university courses in creative writing or journalism schools are a help in learning to write and I have to tell them I don't know. I never took any. But then I never took courses in anything.

Enclose Self-addressed Envelope

I just wrote – and wrote – and wrote. Up every morning at five, banging on an old rickety typewriter until school time. Nobody to bother me but our cat, Jonesy, who developed a bad habit of springing onto my back as I sat hunched in front of the typewriter and holding on with all claws. I'd pitch him over onto the couch where he'd sit glowering at me, tail twitching, and go on writing.

After dinner at night I'd try again if I weren't out coaching a baseball game, refereeing a game of basketball, directing a play or speaking to a church Young People's group. But after a day's teaching I had little mental energy left for writing and had to drive myself. I had one rule that I didn't break: finish the story, get it in the mail. Sooner or later something would have to break.

Two good things happened during these first months. The post office changed hands and Aileen became pregnant.

Next to Smith's store and between it and the restaurant was a vacant lot. It was full of weeds and old tin cans and looked as though it would remain vacant forever. Nobody was building anything in the mid-Thirties. But one day, much to the surprise of the Main Street regulars, a four-horse team pulled into the lot from the lane behind, dragging on skids an old wooden shack. It was battered and broken with tar-covered sides and a flat, slanting roof. The windows were smashed, the door gone.

Two of the local carpenters went to work on it, however, and repaired most of the damage. A coat of paint made it look almost presentable. I discovered why it had been brought there on one of my trips to the post office. Nathan Smith was alone in his store and he was furious.

"There is nothing, absolutely nothing, these people won't do!" he fumed as soon as I entered.

By "these people" I knew he meant his arch enemies, the French Canadians.

"But this . . . this . . . is the lowest yet. It's the ultimate in . . . in . . ." He was lost for words.

It turned out he'd had a visitor from the federal post office that very morning who'd informed him that it was a new policy not to have the post office in his store.

"Why?" he had demanded.

"Well there have been complaints. The French Canadians —and the Ukrainians, too—claim that they are treated badly in here."

"They're treated like anybody else."

"Well . . . there have been complaints."

"What are you going to do about it?"

"Well, we plan to move the post office out of here into a building of its own."

"You want me to erect a building?"

"No. There isn't space for one on the main street now . . . and the post office has to be on the main street. But there's this building next door . . ."

Smith could scarcely continue his recital of the crime. "You see what he did . . . you see . . . ? Got a lot of his pea-soup friends to write to the Department complaining about how I treated them. Then he moves that ramshackle shack onto the only vacant lot on the street. It's as plain as the nose on your face. They're getting it because they're political heelers!"

I couldn't believe this, of course. Danny Beltier was simply the better man for the job. But he had terrible luck. Shortly after the post office was moved into the little building, the place caught fire and burned to the ground. Fortunately there was no loss of mail or vital documents as the fire happened at night when there was little mail in the building and; besides, Danny had been working late that night in the hardware store across the street and had, at great personal risk, rescued everything of value from the building.

Then, as a temporary measure, he established the post office in the hardware store. He built in a separate door where one of the big front windows had been, so that customers wouldn't have to go into his store to get their mail. And he built a nice counter and put in shiny new boxes. It was very handy for Danny, too.

It was more interesting going for the mail now, too, because although he was a highly intelligent man in every respect Danny Beltier was almost blind.

Watching him sort mail for you was as good as a show. He would hold each letter within an inch of his thick glasses and slide it across like a man eating a cob of corn, moving his lips as he did so. He accomplished this with such speed and dexterity that he could sort the mail at least as fast as Smith had ever done.

More important, from my point of view, Danny was tremendously interested in my progress as a writer. Whereas Smith had shown nothing but sullen suspicion as to why so many manila envelopes were going back and forth to New York, Chicago, Philadelphia, Danny was fascinated.

"Don't you worry," he'd say. "Some of these days the story won't come back. You'll see." And each time that one did he was so disappointed that he could scarcely hand it to me. I swore him to secrecy, of course, because I didn't want the people of Wannego to think I was a nut altogether.

"Why?" he asked. "I should think you'd be proud of the fact that you're a writer."

A writer! That was the first time anyone had ever called me that. I didn't go about telling other people that I was a writer. I couldn't. But the realization that at least one man in town called me a writer was a great boost to my spirits.

For I had learned one important thing about the trade of writing. It is the loneliest occupation in the world. You work alone – always alone. Talking to others about what you are doing won't help much because talking is easier than writing and given half a chance any writer will talk his story rather than write it. It's a lonely occupation even for an established writer in a city. For a beginner, in a small Saskatchewan town, it is like being in solitary confinement.

At least it would have been without my wife. Everybody, I guess, must have somebody who believes he can accomplish the impossible. Somebody he can complain to, enthuse with, and even swear at, if necessary. Aileen was then, as she is now, the perfect wife for a writer. Her understanding and patience were complete. With that sure, confident way that women have she knew that some day we would make it. She had no nasty, mean, niggling doubts like the ones that plagued me. She was sure.

By this time Aileen had become considerably pregnant and we were glad. We were so poor that if at the end of the month we had sixty cents left over from our $60.00 cheque it was a cause for jubilation. There was no doctor in the town to provide all that pre-natal care that women need. We had absolutely no idea where we'd get the money for baby carriage, crib, clothes or even diapers. Our water supply was so wretched that washing diapers daily or even bathing a kid would mean back-breaking chores. But just the same we were glad.

Why?

Several reasons. We'd both come from large families where brothers and sisters had been reasonably compatible. Aileen had a great love for babies – anybody's babies, and let's face it, we still had that ridiculous pre-population-explosion idea that raising a family was a worthy thing to do. We actually felt proud that we were going to produce a human being.

In due course of time our first child was born. Aileen went to Saskatoon for the last week so as to be close to the doctor and when she went to the hospital Harry King gave me the day off to go in and be with her. The baby was a girl, healthy and whole. And when I saw her I felt good. No rejection slip here. But I had to take the train back to Wannego that afternoon. Harry didn't believe in pampering his staff.

Enclose Self-addressed Envelope

And it was then that it finally happened. I sold my first short story. What's more, the acceptance letter was accompanied by a cheque and that nearly ended me in Wannego.

I have to go back a bit here. After months of writing stories for *Esquire*, *Liberty*, the *Saturday Evening Post*, *Scribners Magazine* and various other class magazines and getting back nice, clean, crisp rejection slips, I decided on a new tack. I would begin with the lesser markets, something in the manner of a neophyte hunter starting on gophers and working up to lions. Now to find some gophers.

In a copy of the *Writers' Digest* – which was full of helpful hints for beginners – I learned of the newspaper syndicates. "These markets may pay less than the top markets," the item said, "but they are considerably easier to break into." The magazine was always talking of "breaking into" markets and it gave the beginner a nice feeling of putting a broad shoulder against the door of adversity and crashing through.

The syndicate they liked best was the McClure Newspaper Syndicate. The address was given along with the information that they would send writers copies of recent stories they'd bought so that he could study their length, format, style and so on. So I sent for, and they sent to, and much to my surprise I discovered the names of some well-known writers attached to these stories. They were very much in the style of the *Liberty* Short-shorts, a format which I already had studied assiduously.

Hitler was much in the news then, of course, and so was the Nazi Bund in America. They were wearing swastikas on their shoulders and harassing Jews and I got the idea for a story about a Bund member who'd been badly wounded during a demonstration and needed a blood transfusion immediately. The only donor with his type of blood available was Jewish. The denouement – all of these stories had great denouements – came when the recovering Nazi learned that he now had Jewish blood.

I got a letter back from McClure's almost immediately saying they liked my story fine but that somebody else had already used this idea. How about another story? Another story! I had a million of them! But such are the cantankerous caprices of memory that I can't remember what this next one was about.

When I got back to town and went to the post office wicket for my mail Danny Beltier was grinning all over. I was just about to tell him about the baby when he handed me a letter with a celluloid window in the front.

"How about this?" he said.

"Another rejection slip?"

"Nothing doing. This is the kind of letter they send cheques in!"

A cheque! The first I'd ever received as a writer. I stood there holding the thin envelope in my hand afraid to open it. The article about the syndicates had said they paid less than the top markets. Well, less than One Thousand Dollars was Nine Hundred Dollars. Or even Five Hundred Dollars. Hell, I'd settle for a Hundred Dollars, I told myself, but I knew I was just hedging. It couldn't be as little as *One* hundred dollars.

"Aren't you going to open it?" Danny said, grinning. He was as excited as I.

But it isn't so easy to open a letter that might change your life. That might contain news that will rescue you from poverty and frustration. Fame and fortune came suddenly for writers. I knew this from biographies of Edgar Rice Burroughs and Jack London – oh, almost any writer you want to mention. Fame and fortune! It's no wonder I hesitated to open that envelope.

And then I did. And it contained a cheque, just as I had hoped, crisp and brownish and official, attached to a letter of acceptance. And the amount stamped into that cheque so that it could never be tampered with was $5.00.

"Well?" Danny enquired, and I tossed the cheque on the

counter in front of him. He picked it up and ran it in front of his eyes. I knew what he was thinking. Five dollars for all this work! For spending every minute of your spare time hunched over a typewriter, for study and planning and rewriting and more rewriting. For hope and faith and confidence. Five lousy dollars and a story published in the weekend supplement of the *Milwaukee Journal*. This is fame and fortune?

I guess this is the moment that really separates the reasonable from the unreasonable, the sensible from the insane, the rational from the blindly stubborn. Rejection slips you can take. You say – well, that editor doesn't know a good story when he sees it, or the story was never read, or they had another story like it, and you know that some day somebody will recognize your worth and your story will sell.

But to sell a story, have it read and appreciated, finally to break through the great wall of indifference, to enter into the world of payment for them, and then get five lousy stinking bucks. It just plain wasn't worth it. Any sensible person could see that. Now was the time to quit and try something more practical – like taking a course in show-card printing, or learning to play the piano in ten easy lessons, or raising chinchillas in your basement, or studying for a lucrative civil service position, or becoming proficient in the growing field of electronics. Hell, the publications were full of pleasant ways of bettering your station in life with half the work of learning to write.

I must admit that, standing there with that five-dollar cheque in my hand, I felt like quitting all right.

"By the way," I said. "Our baby was born this morning. A girl. Eight pounds, two ounces."

Danny reached through the wicket and grabbed my hand. "Now," he said, "you can buy new shoes for the baby."

Then I knew what I must do with this money. The only thing that could possibly restore my perspective. "To hell with shoes," I said, beginning to feel better already. "I'm

going to get a good bottle of scotch and I'm going to celebrate my success. Are you with me?"

"I sure as hell am," Danny said. "We'll have it at my
house. I'll get Vincent and Maurice and Jean and a few
others and we'll have a big one. We'll celebrate the new
baby and the new cheque."

The people he mentioned were all his friends and all
French Canadian. Vincent Denis was the municipal secretary, Maurice DeSante was the accountant in the bank, Jean
Bouchard was an insurance broker. There were more. A
couple of farmers, assorted nieces and nephews – including
a buxom, bosomy brunette I'd never seen before but who
was very friendly.

This was my first real association with French Canadians.
Like most other good Canadian WASPs, I'd had no direct
contact with them and therefore harboured an attitude of
suspicion and dislike. For one thing they talked French and,
after my dismal experiences with that language, I had a
strong suspicion that anybody who spoke it must be pretty
devious. Since my father had once been an active Orangeman, I'd heard some of the stories of how the Catholics were
taking over the country, and God knows I'd heard enough
from Smith about what liars, cheats, and generally dirty
bastards all Frenchmen were.

I didn't care. At this point I felt reckless.

There is certainly one thing to be said for getting drunk
with people; you get to know them. The party started up at
Danny Beltier's house and his tall, graceful, dark-eyed wife
welcomed me and my bottle of scotch with a big hug. That
was a good beginning.

As each of the others arrived with their wives, I realized
that when they said party they meant party. Each brought a
bottle of booze and some had taken a few nips before they
arrived. They greeted me like a friend of long standing,
enfolded me in warm embraces and insisted that I have a
drink from their bottle. Everybody was glad about the baby.

I'd never seen anything like this before. I'd been on parties with my Anglo-Saxon friends, but they tended to be rather stiff and furtive affairs, degenerating gradually into drunken brawls. Like most other Canadians of that time, we didn't know how to drink. Having been instructed from infancy that alcoholic beverages were tools of the devil – not something to enhance enjoyment and make life good, but rather something to degrade and destroy – we went about drinking guiltily, secretly, defensively and stupidly. And since we'd already taken the first step towards perdition we figured we might as well go all the way, and so we did crazy things like breaking furniture and fighting.

But this was drinking for fun. For enjoyment. For ecstasy. For gaiety and frolic. We danced and laughed and patted each other and, for the first time in public, I emerged from my school-teacher shell. I lost my stiffness, my reserve, my foolish notions. It was fun to hug and kiss the beautiful brunette without being expected to take her into the bedroom. I also learned that I was a very funny fellow when properly lubricated, and that when people finally got through to me they tended to like me. I developed a lot that night, as a person and also as a writer.

I also nearly got fired from my job. I was not then, nor ever have been, what is described as a good drinker. In fact I am a bad drinker. I tend to get very very happy and very very reckless. So it was that when the party had reached the stage that we were marching from house to house and singing, I decided to pay a visit to Mr. McElvey, the bank manager who, you will remember, was also a member of the school board.

Now Mr. McElvey didn't actually disapprove of French Canadians. He knew that the bank had to deal with them and that it was necessary to have an accountant who could speak French – God knows he'd never learn the crazy language himself – but apart from that it just happened that he had no French Canadian friends.

Well, as I rollicked up the street with these wonderful people we passed his house and I somehow got the idea that it was incumbent upon me to climb up on McElvey's front porch roof and sing "Alouette" through his bedroom window.

"You can't do that," Maurice DeSante protested half-heartedly. "It's two o'clock in the morning!"

"And everybody know," said his petite wife who was the only member of the group with any accent, "that these Anglaise are never awake after ten."

"But what if they are making love?" somebody asked.

This brought a considerable laugh from the group and it was obvious they considered that WASPs don't make love, at least not in the sense that they thought of it.

I don't think I ever would have gone any further in this – and I soon wished I hadn't – if somebody hadn't spotted a ladder lying beside the house, put it up to the veranda and said, "Voila!" So up I went, unsteadily, and got onto the veranda roof which was steeper than I'd thought. Gingerly on hands and knees I crawled up to the big double window and began to sing, loudly, drunkenly, and off-key.

Then I was aware of a strange thing. There was no noise behind me. The laughter and banter that had been there had all gone. I looked down on the dark street and it was empty. My friends too were all gone.

Instead of them I made out a dark figure coming down the street. It turned in at the gate. It was Banker McElvey who had obviously been out at a party himself and who was just returning. And there I was, the drunken teacher perched on the porch of the member of the school board.

My mind raced over possible courses of action. I might jump down on top of him and knock him over so that he'd be so stunned he wouldn't see who it was running down the street. No. I might really hurt him. I might jump off the side of the veranda and run around the side of the house. No, I'd probably break a leg or at least sprain an ankle. I even considered diving off the veranda head first and ending it all right there, but the thought of my wife and new baby deterred me.

So I just sat there and looked down foolishly at the figure below. And he looked up at me.

"Braithwaite!" McElvey roared in a big voice.

"Yeah."

"What in hell are you doing sitting on my porch roof singing French Canadian songs, off-key?"

"Well . . . it uh . . . seemed like a good idea. Now I'm not so sure."

"Come down."

So I came down the ladder, which he held for me, and when I reached the bottom McElvey looked at me and said, "That's a hell of a way to sing!"

I had no answer for that. It wasn't the first time my singing had been criticized. But it did seem a little strange that he should be concerned with the quality of my voice at a time like this.

Because I couldn't think of anything else to say, I blurted, "My wife had a baby today. A girl."

"She did? Congratulations! Come on in, I'll buy you a drink. I'll also show you how those songs should be sung. My wife's away, too."

So we went in and it turned out that he was as high as I was and that under the influence, instead of climbing porches, he sang French-Canadian songs. And sang them, and sang them, and sang them. For hours I sat there and drank his whiskey and listened to these songs. He also liked to teach other people how to sing.

Then he became serious and told me how it was being a banker. "These farmers around here think I'm some kind of Shylock because I won't lend them any money. Hell, it's not my money. The bank inspectors come around and rake me over the coals for not collecting what is out. If I lend money on land – what good is land? Who wants it? The bank owns more land than it knows what to do with now. They don't realize what I'm up against."

It was a sad story. I wished he'd go back to singing.

When I finally got out of there it was four in the morning. I walked down the dusty road and then along the cracked sidewalk to the hotel. "Gosh," I said to myself, "Bankers sure do have a miserable time of it."

Enclose Self-addressed Envelope

The worst thing that happened to me during my term at Wannego was not the rejection slips, nor the small pay for a story sold, nor the humiliation of poverty. No, the very worst thing was umpiring a ladies' softball game.

It happened during the July First Sports Day, and in order to properly appreciate the tension and stress of the occasion you must understand something about the annual sports day of a prairie town.

Each town has one and it is a combination of the Mardi-gras, the Summer Olympics and the World Series all rolled into one. It's more than that, actually. It's excitement of such a high pitch that people enter a hypnotic state where all normal modes of behaviour disappear on the hot prairie wind and are replaced by sheer, unadulterated madness.

In the first place, the sports day is always held in the spring or early summer. And spring in Saskatchewan is a wild time. The winter has been six months long, frightfully cold, terribly restricting and unbelievably miserable. In spring, horses, cattle and people dash out of the confinement of their abodes, sniff the air, kick up their heels, gallop madly about and indulge in sports days.

Each town in a district has its special day. Hanley, for instance, always had its sports day on the Twenty-fourth of May, and it was always referred to simply as "The Twenty-fourth." Other towns staked out their claims to other week-ends. In Wannego it was always July First.

July First had several advantages not enjoyed by other days. It was late enough in the season for all spring work to be finished. School kids were released from bondage. The weather was almost sure to be hot – a condition essential to a good sports day. Besides, it was a national holiday with flags flying and bands playing, a great extra incentive to get drunk.

As soon as the snow had gone and the first crocuses were poking up in the pasture, preparations for "The First" began. Mothers dug out patterns, bought cloth and sewed like crazy on new dresses for daughters. Merchants painted store fronts, the livery barn operator hauled away the winter's accumulation of manure. Endless meetings were held and committees appointed. The Ladies' Aid and the Lady Elks laid their plans to best each other in the quantity of hotdogs and pop to be sold in their booths. The bootleggers ran extra batches. Ruby bought a new gingham dress and took a bath.

My own involvement was complete. Along with the other teachers, I worked with our local athletes, digging pits for kids to leap into, staking off race tracks and filling in gopher holes, drilling the tiny tots in the intricacies of the sack and three-legged races. Besides this I was in charge of the senior boys' baseball team.

And baseball was the big, super-duper attraction of the Sports Day. They play good baseball in prairie towns. Most kids start pitching balls around as soon as they can walk. Every school and town has a good team.

There would be four tournaments going simultaneously. The men's senior baseball tournament, the ladies' senior softball tournament, the school boys' baseball and the girls' softball tournaments. The three lesser tournaments drew their small coterie of fans – relatives and friends of the players, mostly, while the senior baseball always drew the biggest crowd.

Even in the Thirties prizes for the senior baseball were high, with up to five hundred dollars for first money. The knockout competition began early in the day and went on until the sun had sunk below the prairie horizon. Old-timers pulled their trucks or buggies in along the baselines and never left for the whole day. I can still see those cars and trucks nosed in against the chickenwire fence that stretched along the baselines and the farmers in their blue serge suits visiting back and forth, commenting on the play and re-membering when – oh such a short time ago – they them-selves were full of pep and ginger standing out there at shortstop giving the old pepper talk.

But it's about one of the lady softball players that I must speak, since it was she who brought about my downfall. Her name was Julia King and she had a preferred position so far as I was concerned since she was the wife of the principal of the school. A solid woman, Julia was. She'd been raised on a farm up in the Cut Knife district, where there were a lot of Italians. She was what you might call hefty Italian and in her veins flowed the blood of the true Romans. One of her delights, to demonstrate her strength, was to pick Harry up and hold him in her arms like a baby. She'd wrist-wrestle with the men on the kitchen table and beat any of them. And when she got into her softball uniform with the black shorts so tight around her ample backside to be indecent, leg muscles bulging and big breasts jouncing, she was a formidable sight.

Harry King doted on her. She was his idea of the perfect woman. None of your soft, namby-pamby females about her – Harry particularly detested namby-pambyism – and he delighted in the fact that she could out-work and out-fight any man he knew.

Harry's other great passion was ladies' softball. Coaching the team being his one community project, he spared no time or effort in producing the best team of the district. He was strict, stern and demanding. A girl or woman had to measure up to be on Harry's team. She had to play the game with all she had for Harry was a keen competitor, dedicated to winning at all costs. And he always won. In the ten years he'd been teaching in this general area he'd taught in three different towns and in each of them his team had won the tournament every single year.

So the great day came. "The First." Canada's birthday, celebrating that other day nearly seventy years earlier when the Fathers of Confederation had set their signatures to a document making Canada one nation.

I don't remember any patriotic celebrations or parades or pageants or bosoms swelling with pride or speeches by politicians. And I really don't know if this was because people didn't think about it or just didn't care. Certainly there was little in the mid-Thirties to make us proud of being Canadians.

But a Sports Day, now. That was a different batch of dandelion greens entirely. All the patriotism and pride was centered in the local community. Beat the other towns, that was the thing. Show them we could put on a better Sports Day, field a better baseball team, and ladies' softball team, prove that our young men could run faster than their young men. Competition. That was the outlet for our civic pride. And, after all, isn't that what life is all about?

The day dawned bright and clear. There had been some clouds hanging around the horizon the night before and the town had watched them anxiously. Rain could ruin everything. All spring long they'd watched the sky for a sign of rain. Rain that would lay those murderous dust storms, rain that would nourish the growing wheat, rain that would mean the difference between some crop and no crop at all.

"Just like it to rain on 'The First' when we haven't had a sprinkle all spring," Mrs. Polonski lamented. But just at sundown on June 30 the sun broke through the clouds, suffusing the northwestern horizon with a fine red glow and shooting crimson fingers out through the clouds. And the great red ball of the sun sat there on the prairie like a straw stack on fire.

"Red sky in the morning, sailor take warning. Red sky at night, sailor's delight," Old Dad Trainor said, and everybody felt better. Dad was the oldest man in town and one of the most active. He'd never been a sailor, everybody knew

Women Shouldn't Play Baseball

that, but his prediction was the one all wanted to hear and so they believed him to a man.

Everybody in Wannego was up early that morning. So much to do! Dresses to finish for the dance. Last-minute decorations to be put on the Ladies Aid booth. Lime to be spread along the base paths of the various diamonds, and cow pads fresh laid by Birkenshire's cow, that never could be kept tied up, to be cleared away. Didn't want a repetition of last year, when Doody Wingate in his new uniform had missed second base and slid into a fresh cow flap.

By nine o'clock teams were arriving from the other towns. The Aberdeen bunch had brand new uniforms again. Aberdeen was in a pocket of that heavy gumbo soil and seemed to have a crop no matter how little rain fell. Teams from Lanigan, Humboldt, Kinistino, Melfort, Star City, Wakaw, and one from Hanley which was really the one to watch because they had won the tournament at Watrous the week before with the help of a coloured pitcher they'd imported from south of the border. If they had him again they'd be hard to beat.

Dad Tranior scanned each team for what he called "ringers." These were imported players from the u.s. hired for a hundred dollars or so to play for that one day only. Trouble was nobody knew what these strangers could do. They might belt the ball out of the township every time at bat, or strike out every batter who faced them.

Dad reported on each team that arrived. "There's a guy I never seen before with that Wakaw bunch," he stated. "Little runt with horn-rimmed specs. Don't like the look on it."

Sure enough when Wakaw took the field for the first game the little runt with specs was on the mound. And from the first ball he threw a groan went up from the regulars in the bleachers. It came in there so fast and so straight that the batter just plain didn't see it. This guy spells trouble, they said.

And they were absolutely right. The little guy did spell trouble with a capital T. Not only did he strike out batter after batter, but he took to taunting his victims. He'd deliberately throw three balls and then announce in a loud voice that "now I'm coming to get you-all!" The next three pitches would breeze over the plate so fast that the batter had no chance. And after each futile swing the little guy with specks would throw back his head and laugh.

As the batters came away from the plate, grim lipped, shaking their hands, it was clear that they were planning a moment of reckoning somewhere, somehow. If not with the bat, then by some other means. Before the day was half over everybody in the town was muttering about the "little guy with the specs." He, they all agreed, would most certainly get his.

It was a perfect day for baseball. Hot as only a July prairie day can be hot. By noon the temperature was 98° in the shade – and there was no shade. On the ball diamonds, big patches of wet were appearing on the players' uniform shirts. The sun sat high in the big sky and poured down its heat. And everybody loved it.

Farmers removed the jackets of their blue serge suits and hung them carefully in the back of the Essex or Overland. They rolled up the sleeves of their white shirts, removed collars and ties and tucked in the collar bands. If there is any greater fun than sitting in your shirt sleeves watching a baseball game and soaking up the heat I don't know what it is.

My senior boys' team did quite well. We took the Aberdeen school and the Kinistino school, but then we ran into a "packed" team from Star City and they beat us 4-2. We knew it was a packed team, all right. Why some of those guys had left high school three years before. But when we protested, their principal, a crook if I ever saw one, said that the ringers were back in school taking extra subjects. "They haven't anything else to do," he said. "So we feel they might as well be back in school." This caused great anger among our players. Not so much because the others had done it, but because we hadn't thought of it.

Being knocked out of the tournament gave me a few minutes to spare. I found Aileen, who was pushing Beryl around to her second-hand wicker carriage that Mrs. Shirley had given us. We talked to people and visited and watched the senior baseball for a while.

And then, just after we'd had a hurried supper, Harry King caught me.

"What are you doing?" he wanted to know.

"Well . . . for the moment . . . nothing."

"Good. Then you can umpire the final game of the ladies' softball, between us and Humboldt."

"Uh . . . well . . . I thought George Henshaw was your referee."

"That guy! He damned near robbed us of the game against Lanigan. We had one of their runners cold at home and he called her safe. No, we need a good referee for this game and you're the best there is. Better be there a little before seven," he said, and left.

Now it is clear evidence of my colossal gullibility that I didn't see what my principal was up to. What he really meant – "We can be sure that in any close decision you'll give us the nod or I'll bloody well know the reason why."

All I did was blush becomingly and say that . . . oh I wasn't that good, but I'd be glad to umpire the game.

Aileen looked sad when I said this. I guess any woman hates to see her husband led into the lion's den.

When Harry left I said to Aileen, "I think I'll put on my grey flannels and my new two-tone shoes."

I had acquired the two-tone shoes only the week before and I was inordinately proud of them. They were black and white, I remember, and far the most exciting shoes I have ever owned. I guess I really loved those shoes. God knows I couldn't afford the $4.95 they had cost me, but when I saw them in Peter Nikoluk's store I couldn't resist them.

"But it'll be terribly dusty out there on the diamond," Aileen protested further, "and your new shoes will be ruined."

"I think I'll wear my blue blazer, too," I added.

"But, Max . . . it will get covered with dust. Why do you want to . . ." And then she got a look in her eye that young wives sometimes get when they want to be most unreasonable. "Oh, I see. Of course. All those girls bouncing around the bases in their shorts!"

"That's not it at all. It's a matter of authority."

"Hah!"

"It is. If I go out there in this outfit . . . well, nobody's going to pay any attention. But in my grey flannels and blue blazer and two-tone shoes. . . ."

"You'll be the Beau Brummell of the diamond."

"Oh for God sake. That's just plain stupid!"

Well, the word "stupid" always does it. I suppose, syllable for syllable, it's the most powerful word in the language for settling arguments. Husbands use it when they're backed into a corner and can fight their way out in no other way. Wives use it but in a different way. They work around until they get their husbands to use it and then they say—"Stupid! So now I'm stupid!"

Anyway, promptly at five minutes to seven I presented myself at the ladies' softball diamond. Aileen hadn't come. She said she hated to see people get killed.

There was a surprisingly large crowd on hand, I thought, and a very intense one, too. I didn't realize it then but the rivalry between Wannego and Humboldt was of long standing. Many times before they had met in the finals and each time Wannego had won. This time, however, Humboldt was sure they were going to win. I soon found out why.

Since there was only one umpire available – the other men showed a peculiar reluctance to have anything to do with ladies' softball – I took up my position behind the pitcher. This would enable me to see all the bases reasonably well and, besides, it meant I didn't have to rumple my blue blazer with a chest protector.

Humboldt took the field first and their new pitcher took her place in front of me and I couldn't take my eyes off her. My God what a build! Gina Lollabrigida, Elizabeth Taylor, Marilyn Monroe and Helen of Troy. She was all of them rolled into one gorgeous package. All of the ladies' uniforms were brief, but hers was one-thousand-per cent briefer. When she wound up to take her warm-up pitches I damned near had to leave the diamond.

Finally I croaked, "Play Ball!" and the game got under way.

It soon became apparent that not only was Olga Stevenson the most beautiful thing that ever decorated a pitcher's mound, but she could also throw that ball like a bullet.

Julia King was the lead-off batter for Wannego. She held the bat like a butcher about to poleax a steer. Her eyes flashed, her lips drew into a snarl, and she crowded the plate as though she owned it. The first pitch whizzed within six inches of her slightly bulging belly, but caught the inside of the plate. She leaped back like a startled heifer and I bellowed "Strike One."

The cry that arose on the prairie air then was like unto that which must have emerged from the Indians at the Battle of Batoche. It was part scream, part howl, part roar, and all rage. The predominate words would have to be "Robber!" "Blind man!" "Cheat!" "Liar!"

On top of that, Julia King was advancing towards me from home plate brandishing her bat, and from the corner of my eye I saw her spouse coming at me from the bench. I'd never seen him like this before. Gone was the smooth, cool, slightly detached image. Instead was a monster, a Dr. Jekyll, eyes flashing, arms waving, head jerking, mouth frothing. "What in bloody hell do you think you're doing, you dumb-bell?" To be called a dumb-bell by one's principal is disconcerting in the extreme. I realized I was in big trouble.

To make matters worse Olga turned towards me, flashed her most gorgeous smile and purred, "Never mind them, Handsome, just call them as you see them." Her remarks were lost in the roar of the crowd, but her smile could be seen and interpreted for a country mile.

The rest of the game is a hodgepodge of noise, vituperation, and horror to me. Confronted with a situation like this I am afflicted with a condition – well-known to my friends – which can only be described as a Braithwaite stubbornness. Instead of leaning ever so slightly in favour of the home team – as any fool who knew which side his cheque was signed on would do – I moved slightly in favour of the other side. All the ties and really close ones I called for the Humboldt team. Nobody was ever going to accuse me of local favouritism.

It's a funny thing about women in competitive games. I don't think they should play them at all. They are far too competitive – too emotional. In the heat of battle they completely lose the veneer of civilized beings and revert to the savage. Imagine girls playing professional hockey, for instance. The game would be one long fight from beginning to end. Women with hockey sticks in their hands! Running into each other. Bumping each other about. It would be murder!

So, because of the emotion-charged nature of the game and my unreasonable attitude, things went from bad to worse. Harry King tried to remove me from the game, but the Humboldt team threatened to walk off the diamond if he did. Pitch by pitch, out by out, decision by decision, I was digging my grave in Wannego, betraying my friends, alienating my wife. And, such is that nature of Braithwaite stubbornness that I was powerless to stop it.

The climax came, as all good climaxes should, in the

ninth inning. The dread had been growing in me all through the game that at the very end some decision of mine would decide the outcome. It was more than a dread; it was a premonition, a certainty that it would happen. And sure enough it did.

Without any help from me, the Wannego girls, under the expert direction of Harry King, had managed to get a three-run lead, which they held until the last of the ninth. Then Ruthie Honchuck, who was pitching for Wannego, blew up. She just started missing the plate, and the more she tried the worse she got. Then she began to cry and pout, which was only made worse by Harry's stern admonitions from the sidelines. Before she could be replaced she'd let in three runs and the winning run was on third base.

Finally Harry pulled his pitcher and replaced her with his wife Julia, whom he always said was good for one inning in every game. Oh, I can still see it – and feel it. Julia striding across from her usual place at first base and taking her place on the mound. If ever determination was written into a visage it was written into hers. She tossed the ball up and down in her hand as though it were a bomb. Then she turned and looked at me and if ever hatred was concentrated in a gaze it was concentrated in that one.

Julia faced that plate as though everything she ever wanted in life was centred in that small slab of wood. Come to think of it, it was. At that one, intense moment she wanted so badly to win that if she'd been offered a choice between losing that game and losing her whole fortune there's no doubt in my mind which she'd have chosen. Such is the competitive urge.

All her energies, all her concentration went into those pitches. The first six of them were strikes and the batters had no chance. Thank God, I breathed, this amazon of a woman will rescue me from my predicament. I will be saved.

Then disaster.

The next batter was none other than that gorgeous piece of feminine pulchritude, Olga Stevenson. Here was her chance to win her own ball game. But she didn't really have much chance. The first two pitches whizzed past her so fast she never got the bat off her shoulder. From where I stood they looked like strikes and so I announced in a loud, firm voice. Julia even turned and smiled on me. Harry yelled from the sidelines, "Good eye, Ump!" My cup of happiness was brimming over.

But it's often been said that a ball game is never really in the bag until the last strike has been thrown. High as a kite with self-confidence and contempt, Julia took the ball and glared down at the batter. And here psychology reared its ugly head. Instead of glaring back at Julia, Olga smiled her dazzling smile and said in her beautiful Swedish accent for all to hear, "All right, Baggy Pants, let's see the next one!"

Now if there was anything Julia King couldn't be accused of, on the diamond or off, it was having baggy pants. Her face went white as the ball in her hand. Harry, who had heard the remark and knew his wife, leaped to his feet waving his arms for time, but it was too late. Julia had let the ball go – straight for her tormentor's head.

It was all very confused after that, with much rushing and shouting and screaming. As nearly as I could make out, Olga ducked her head and brought the bat up for protection. The ball hit the bat and dropped onto the diamond, trickling towards the pitcher. Olga sprinted for first base; the runner at third lumbered towards home. Julia leaped to field the ball and fell on her face. But she managed to get it and from a sitting position tossed it to first, which was really the only play.

Like the good umpire I was, I had also sprinted for first base so as to be close to the play. With eagle eyes I watched the base and with ears keen as fallow deer I listened for the smack of the ball in the first baseman's glove. They came simultaneously, exactly together. Now, as a kid playing baseball, we always used to say that a tie goes to the runner. To this day I don't know whether or not this is the rule, but I believed it then. So, without even a second's thought, I waved my arms flat out and bellowed, "SAFE!"

The game was over. Humboldt had won. And every one of those Wannego players — and their sisters — and their brothers — and their parents — made for me. And I ran. Like a cowardly poltroon, I sprinted across that field heading for the sanctuary of the schoolhouse. But there was a fence between me and safety and when I tried to scramble through it the barbs caught first on the back of the jacket and then on the seat of the pants. As I jerked to get free there was a horrible, long ripping sound and both were ruined. But I got through and made it to the school and got in the door and locked it. My pursuers had given up anyway, all except Julia King, who tugged at the handle of the door and screamed and screamed. Her husband came and led her away, finally, sobbing as though her heart would break. She had lost the game!

At the conclusion of every Sports Day came the Sports Day dance. Nothing during the year could compare with it for the size of the crowd, the quality of the music, or the amount of home-brew and store booze consumed in the cars parked outside the Opera House.

After my disgrace on the softball diamond, I had little inclination to expose myself to more abuse. We would not, I decided, go to the dance. But Aileen had other ideas. This was the first big affair that had come along since Beryl's arrival and she was anxious to go. Besides, she hadn't missed a Sports Day dance in years. In Hanley, where she had grown up and where her father, a leading member of the Elk's Lodge, had practically run the event, missing a Sports Day dance was like missing Christmas. She had arranged that Mrs. Polonski would look in on Beryl, and she had made a dress that was all fluffy and frilly. She looked beautiful. I had to press up the trousers of my old blue serge and make them do. Anyway, I had the two-tone shoes.

Everybody was there, from babies in arms to grandparents. Baby sitters hadn't yet been invented; besides, no good parent would deprive their infants the fun of a Sports Day dance. The same with grandparents. The idea that they should stay home and engage in their own feeble pastimes never entered anybody's head. Those who didn't dance sat on benches along the wall and watched those who did. Those who wanted to dance simply got up and danced. The steps were the same as they'd danced when young – fox trots, waltzes, the flea hop. Children danced with grandparents, sons with mothers, fathers with daughters. The generation gap? Nobody had ever heard of it.

All the ball players were there, some still in uniform, others in zoot suits with wide-lapel jackets and tapering trousers. All the females, old and young, had new dresses for the occasion. Scrubbed and powdered and perfumed they were, and on the prowl. Now was the time to meet new men, now was the chance to show that local boy friend who'd been taking you for granted that he wasn't the only pebble on the beach. This was the night for excitement, gaiety, abandonment, romance.

The town had hired the best orchestra in the district for the occasion, the Goodales from Floral. There was a piano player, a violinist, a saxophonist, a drummer and a beautiful female singer. I'm telling you when the Goodales played "The Waltz You Saved For Me," there wasn't a foot in the hall that could keep from gliding.

They were good on the fast stuff, too. For "Tiger Rag" they roared the beginning of each line, and in "The Dark Town Strutter's Ball" they strutted around the stage. They had fun caps and special lighting effects and, come to think of it, just about everything modern groups have. Only difference, they played music everybody could dance to.

I had to dance with Julia King. I knew that. But the memory of those flashing eyes and that menacing baseball bat and those shrill threats was strong upon me. I spotted her soon enough, in a most attractive dress she'd made herself. She beamed on me as of old and I invited her to dance. She was as nice as pie. I've always said that it's the uniform that makes cops and hockey players and lady athletes mean. Harry invited me out to his car for a drink of fairly good rye whiskey. We took it straight from the bottle, as was the custom in Saskatchewan in those days, and when I tried to sort of explain about the umpiring thing, he looked at me with that expressionless face of his and said, "Well, you know, it's not winning that counts, but how you play the game."

At the conclusion of each dance all the girls went to one end of the hall or found seats along the side while all the men went to the other end which was close to the door. They'd nip down the steps and out to their cars for a quick one and then be back in time for the next dance.

As usual, some of the ball players from other towns were there without women and, as the liquor glowed in their bellies, they, as usual, became more free and easy with the local girls. The most forthright of all was the little runt with the horn-rimmed specs. His team had won the big money and what with the taunting and all that he'd done during the games he was about as popular with the local boys as a skunk at a picnic.

On top of that, he was dressed, as the girls said, fit to kill. Nobody around there had seen anything quite like it. The lapels were wider, the pants higher, the shirt louder and the shoes flashier than those of anybody else on the floor. And he had a beautiful southern drawl, and manners to go with it that completely captivated the girls. He had a way of inviting them to dance – "I beg your pardon, Ma'am, but would you do me the honour of the next dance?" – which contrasted markedly with the local custom which was simply to stand in front of a girl, grimace, and jerk the head towards the dance floor.

It was plain that there was trouble for somebody in all this.

As the evening wore on the dancers became more and more animated and hot. Windows were thrown open, jackets removed, but to no avail. Perspiration was pouring off the dancers like rain off a roof. There were no square dances – Wannego was much too sophisticated for that – but there were circle two-steps and moonlight waltzes and tag dances. It was a broom dance that finally started the riot.

For those under forty who don't understand the intricacies of the broom dance, I shall explain. Each guy got himself a girl in the usual manner and started dancing. One guy, usually somebody who had something to do with organizing the dance, took a broom in lieu of a partner. It didn't matter what kind of broom since he wasn't going to keep it long anyway.

Well, he'd dance around with this broom and then he'd tag a guy who was dancing with a girl, whereupon the tagged one took the broom and gave up his partner. It was all good-natured and jolly and usually nobody took offence. But again Fate took a hand. For the little guy with the specs got the broom.

Baldy Wail, who was Wannego's star batter, had gone hitless in the final game and had been the target of the little guy's taunts. This was okay. Baldy could take it. But now he was consoling himself with Olga Stevenson. Baldy was big and muscular and handsome. More than one girl in town had felt the weight of his overpowering charm. But now they were out of the running. Olga was the target for tonight.

The little guy had the broom and was cutting capers on the floor. He'd dance around with it and twice he held it with both hands in front of him and leaped over it.

Then he spied Baldy with the beautiful Olga and made for them. With a deep bow and a flourish, he held forth the broom. Instead of taking it, Baldy placed a mammoth hand on the little guy's chest and shoved. The little guy went back but he didn't go over. He leaped forward head first and caught Baldy in the pit of the stomach. The fight was on.

It was a good fight for a while. All the ball players got into it. Not having had enough to drink and with a wife to protect, I left early. We met three Mounties coming in. As we walked down the street an Oldsmobile convertible went roaring by. And who was in it? Why the Little Guy, of course. And who was with him? None other than Olga Stevenson.

That summer we went camping and then we moved to a little house on the outskirts of town. It was our first real home and I guess in many ways we were as happy there as we have ever been. Frustrated, sure, and angry and wild. But we had good friends, enough to eat, a house to ourselves, and – most important – hope for the future.

Soon after the Sports Day and the dance we were faced with summer holidays which meant two months without pay. So we did what young people still do: we moved in with Aileen's folks. They had a house in Saskatoon, but there wasn't really enough room for us so we scraped together enough money to rent camping equipment and announced that we were going to live at Emma Lake for the summer.

"You mean you're going to take a baby who is less than two months old on a camping trip?" Bob Treleaven asked.

We said we didn't think it would hurt her.

And that was all either he or his wife, Amy, ever said on the subject. But naturally they were worried. They were pretty old-fashioned when it came to caring for babies. They believed that they should be protected and loved and comforted when they cried and even rocked to sleep. They believed, too, that babies should be petted and talked to and played with and fed when they were hungry and given comforters to keep them happy. Most of all, babies shouldn't be taken off into the wilds with mosquitoes and black flies and bears and God knows what to molest them.

We, of course, being enlightened, modern parents, knew all that stuff was unnecessary, even harmful. For we were determined to treat our baby with modern scientific methods as laid down by the baby care experts of the Thirties.

This theory, which had a great vogue then, held that parents were actually bad for babies. Too much tender loving care would ruin the tykes for life. Routine, that was the thing. Babies should be fed on schedule at exactly the same time each day and exactly the right amount of a balanced diet. If they were hungry, let them cry. Crying developed the lungs. The same thing applied to sleep-time and waking-time and all other routines. One expert, I remember, went so far as to say the ideal condition for a new baby was probably in a glass cage, safe from the contaminating hands of parents and relatives.

Aileen's folks knew this was a lot of bunk. They didn't know it from reading books or magazine articles; they knew it from raising six children of their own and heaping love and affection on them by the shovelful. But they wouldn't interfere. Partly because they knew it wouldn't do any good – nobody is more stubborn than brand-new, "modern" parents – and partly because they knew we would eventually come to our senses. And of course they were right.

Anyway, we decided to go camping. I rented the full outfit of camping gear and we loaded our stuff, including a bassinet, blankets, baby bath-tub and a million diapers, into the car of Aileen's brother, Cas, who was working at Emma Lake that year and had a girl who was working there, too.

Off we went. We had left some vital piece of equipment in the rooms in Wannego and so, since it was almost on the route to the lake, we decided to stop and get it. But when we got there and tried the door I discovered I'd left the key in Saskatoon. So I decided to crawl in the high window between the rotunda and the closet, which we had been using as a pantry.

Two things about this episode were typical of me: I was an inveterate key-leaver and I always had wretched luck trying to crawl through windows.

Back in my courting days, when Aileen was teaching the

town school near where I was teaching in a rural school, and I was boarding with the Ryan family two miles from town, I'd had my worst experience with windows. Johnny Ryan who, besides being my landlord was the chairman of the school board, was a man of broad understanding. Each evening as soon as dinner was over I'd strike out for town and it would be very late when I returned. Johnny, who got up at four for spring seeding, naturally went to bed very early.

I can still see that farm yard when I walked into it around one or two in the morning and the damned dog, a scruffy farm collie named Boy, would start to bark. Then I'd discover I'd forgotten to take my house key. So I'd bang on the door and Johnny would get up and come shivering in his long flannel nightgown and let me in. He was always so good-natured about it and I always felt so lousy that each time it happened I'd assure him earnestly that I'd never forget my key again.

And, after a number of initial failures, I actually managed it for a while. Then one early morning when I trudged into that yard I remembered that my key was upstairs on the wash stand where I'd set it when I'd changed my pants. Damn it all anyway. I couldn't waken Johnny again, I couldn't. I thought of walking back the two miles to Aileen's boarding house and asking Ken Bentley if I could sleep on his couch. No, I couldn't do that. Sleep in the barn, maybe. Too cold. I decided to crawl in the kitchen window.

This seemed easy. The window was low and wide and when I investigated I discovered somebody had actually left it open about two inches. Great. I'd get in, sneak up the stairs and not disturb anybody. Even Boy was keeping quiet. He just sat there watching me with a stupid grin on his face. I think the rotten beast knew what was going to happen.

Slowly and carefully I raised the window without so much as a sound. Aha, some potted geraniums on the sill.

Five Dollars a Month Rent

Ever so gently I lifted them out and set them on the ground. Then I proceeded to crawl in.

I think I may have mentioned elsewhere that I was never the most agile person in the world. I tended to be a little stiff in my movements and – well, damned clumsy was what I was. I put one foot over the sill and sort of waved it about, feeling for anything like a chair that would make a clatter if shoved over. Nothing. So I gave a little jump with the other foot and shifted my body weight through the window. The foot that was already in came down inside a large pan full of milk that had been set on a low bench to cool. That's why the window had been left open. I tried to hold back but I'd committed myself and my whole weight came down in that milk, which fell with a sickening clatter on the floor.

In trying to pull back I knocked against the stick that was holding up the window and the damned thing came down on my back. I couldn't move. There was the sound of slippered feet on the stairway and a yellow glow came towards me through the kitchen. It was a coal-oil lamp with Johnny Ryan behind it.

"For God sake, Max, he asked, "why didn't you come in through the door?"

"My key," I gasped. "I left the damned thing on the wash stand."

"I know. Margaret found it there when she was dusting your room. I unlocked the door for you. See . . ." He went over and swung the heavy kitchen door open to the night. Then he lifted the window off my back and the two of us mopped up the kitchen floor. You can't leave milk lying around all night – and God but it makes a mess!

I realize that the story of my climbing through the window from the rotunda to our suite may be anti-climactic now, but I'll tell it anyway. It's different from the Ryan episode in that the window was about eight feet from the floor. Since it was still not seven o'clock in the morning, there was nobody in the rotunda.

"All I need," I said to Aileen, who was holding the baby in her arms, and to her brother Cas, "is something to climb up to that window with."

"Why don't we just go on without that kettle," Aileen protested. "You might fall!"

Cas, who was a young man of action, had moved one of the big stuffed leather chairs over under the window and said, "Climb up on the back of that. Then you can reach it."

He was right. From the back of the chair I could reach the window. It wasn't hooked and it swung out nicely. Aileen reminded me of the shelf just inside the window on which was a row of quart sealers filled with cooked pumpkin. The explanation for that is very simple. Pumpkin is cheap; in fact the gardens of Wannego had been full of them the fall before. Somebody had given us four immense ones and being frugal we'd bought a dozen sealers (come to think of it, it was the same grocer who gave us the pumpkin that sold us the sealers) and put enough pumpkin mush to last us – at the rate we used it – for thirty-seven years. Carefully I set the pumpkin jars away from in front of the window and let myself down onto the table. I was in without breaking a thing.

I got the kettle and went to the door to go out, only to remember that with this door you needed a key to open it from the inside. That meant another trip out through the window. Again I was careful not to put any weight on the pumpkin shelf and just had both knees on the window sill when Aileen said, "Oh you might as well get the baby's pink blanket while you are in there."

Why do wives do this?

"But I'm not in there," I argued. "I'm half way out."

"I really need the blanket," she said. "It won't take you a minute."

As a matter of fact it took all the rest of the morning because, in a moment of pique, I put my weight on that damned shelf and the whole thing hit the floor. Stewed pumpkin, I discovered, especially when it's gone rotten, makes a far worse mess and is much harder to clean up than spilt milk.

When we got to the lake we pitched our tent on the edge of the sand beach. Nearby was a huge outdoor fireplace and not far from that a cook kitchen. Everything we needed. Each morning, long before anyone else was up, I would walk back and forth from the lake carrying water, and heat it in a copper boiler on the fireplace. Then I'd wash the diapers and hang them up to dry. Aileen would bathe the baby in the cook kitchen and she usually had a small gallery of other females watching the show. Then we'd put Beryl into her basket, lug it down to the shore, cover it with mosquito net and spend the morning there swimming, goofing off, and keeping the sun out of the baby's eyes. In the afternoon I'd set up the typewriter near the tent and try to do some writing, but my heart wasn't in it. All this depended, of course, on its not ever raining. The drought was good for something.

We spent three great weeks there, far away from any doctor, let alone a pediatrician – come to think of it, they may not have been invented yet – and nobody ever needed one. Doctors are like peanuts; the handier they are, the more you want them.

Then we took the bus back to Wannego. It wasn't a real bus, rather a large sedan whose chassis had been lengthened and a special body built onto it. The driver piled our baby basket, boiler and other paraphernalia on the top of the bus and lashed it securely. We squeezed inside with an assortment of steaming passengers while that bus stopped at every town, village, hamlet and even every crossroad on the way home.

We'd come back to Wannego early because we'd decided to rent a house. Finding a house was no problem – half the houses in town were uninhabited; finding one we could afford was another thing. We looked at some that rented for eight dollars a month and even one that rented for ten. But it was too big and grand for us. It even had running water, and a flush toilet. "It's not so much the rent," Aileen said, "but where would we get the furniture and curtains and rugs for it. (My credit wasn't any good. I tried to borrow fifty dollars from the bank once, and although the manager was a member of the school board and knew I was getting sixty dollars a month regularly, he wouldn't lend it to me.) So we settled on a much smaller house that rented for five dollars a month.

I'll never forget that first house we lived in. It was the sort of house rich people sometimes have off in the bush where they can go to rough it. The house was about twenty feet square with two rooms, a living room and a bedroom. Tacked onto the back was a lean-to which served as a kitchen and in the middle of the kitchen floor was a trap door that led down into a deep, dark, earthen-walled cellar in which there was a huge cistern. Above the cistern was a sink with a pump attached. That was our water system. There was no indoor plumbing, no furnace, and no insulation. It was the coldest house I've ever lived in.

Outside it was wonderful. The yard was about half an acre surrounded by a fence and a caragana hedge. Half the yard was garden where we could grow most of our food, and the garden was surrounded by huge box elder trees that were full of kingbirds. There was only one house within a block of us and that was across what would have been a street if there'd been a street there. The school was within walking distance.

The house needed redecorating in every room and so we made a deal with the owner, Mr. Nikoluk of the general store, that if he would supply the wallpaper and paint we would do the job. We had a whole month to do it in, and a good thing, too. Aileen took Beryl to her grandmother's and left her there. We scrounged an old metal bed from my folks and a good Ostermoor mattress from Aileen's. We already had a stove and a couple of chairs and the cedar chest, which the dray man moved for us for three dollars. We found an old pot-bellied, ornate, rusty heater (behind the blacksmith shop) which the blacksmith gave us. For five dollars down we got an unpainted kitchen set consisting of a gate-legged table and two chairs. To be sure, the living room was bare, but liveable.

We soon discovered that the little house was haunted. Not haunted in a bad way or a noisy way or in a destructive way, but in a nice way. For instance, we'd be working away measuring wallpaper or pasting it or painting the kitchen cupboards when somebody would gently tap us on the shoulder. Then we would look at each other, lay aside our paste and paint, spread a blanket on the floor and make love with the sun streaming in through the curtainless windows and the grasshoppers making music in the grass outside.

But that idyll was spoiled somewhat by a dark, awful, soul-shrivelling fear of having another child. We had one – and we wanted her and needed her. She was essential to our functioning, I'm convinced of that. For whatever else we were, Aileen was a born mother-type and I a born father-type.

But we both knew that another child at that time would be too much for us. We would have to give up the dream and settle down to being as successful as we could in the job we were in. And that would have been horrible.

And so, each month as the fateful date approached, Aileen and I became more and more restive. My eyes were continually asking her the vital question and her eyes were continually avoiding mine, because she didn't have the right answer. And nature would play tricks on us. She would delay a day or two and watch us squirm. And then I'd come home after four and ask, "How are you feeling?" And Aileen would reply with a happy smile, "Terrible!" and we knew we'd been spared another month.

Then would come the month when the right answer

The Night We Stole The Mountie's Car

seemed as though it would never come and we would panic. Somewhere I'd learned that quinine would stop a pregnancy. Quinine and hot baths. So I would sit my poor worried wife in the galvanized washtub in the middle of the floor and bring in near-boiling water by the kettleful and pour it around her. "Can you stand that?"

"No, but keep bringing it. Make it hotter."

Redder and redder she'd get, like a boiled lobster. I don't know if quinine and hot baths will really bring about the longed-for results, but many a time it seemed to work.

I read somewhere, too, that beet juice would do the trick. We had plenty of beets so I boiled a big potful, mashed them up and strained the bloody mess through a flour sack and gave Aileen the juice to drink. Gallons of it she drank, and again it worked. Or at least we thought it worked.

And then, inevitably, would come the month when nothing would work. Each day my eyes would ask the same question, until I could no longer even bear to ask it. It was too cruel. We'd sit down and have that long, awful talk about abortions.

"Where would we ever get one hundred and fifty dollars?" Aileen would ask miserably.

"Borrow it, I suppose. But I don't know who from!"

"We'd have to be careful to keep it from our parents. It would kill them."

It was all so unreal, so horrible, but we knew hundreds of helpless young people were forced into that miserable decision. It's ghastly to contemplate how many potential saviours of mankind – great scientists, enlightened politicians, religious leaders, great musicians, writers – were flushed down toilets or pitched into furnaces during those arid, awful times, before they ever got a chance to draw a breath or feel the touch of a hand. As for ourselves, we managed to stay lucky. Just when we had given up hope, nature stopped playing her little trick – and we would be safe for another month.

Water·was our second greatest problem. Old Shannon came around once a week with a big tank of drinking water from which he filled our small tank for five cents a pail. But we needed a lot of water for washing. It rained enough in the fall to keep the cistern from going dry, but in the winter we had to melt snow. Every Saturday I was up early cutting great chunks of snow from the drifts outside the back door, lugging them into the house and melting them in the copper boiler set on the stove. Then I'd dump the boiling water into the cistern, which meant that I could throw considerably more snow down there and it would gradually melt.

Just behind us was the farm of the Tourniers, a jolly, middle-aged couple who had fourteen children. One of these, Marie, delivered fresh butter and eggs to the door regularly. The butter was always the same price, 25¢ a pound, but the eggs varied, sometimes going down as low as two dozen for a quarter.

As a matter of fact, we lived quite well. The butcher, who was really no butcher at all but just a man who had taken up the trade when there was no more work in his own trade as a carpenter, sold all his beef at the same price – 25¢ a pound. After all, that's the way he bought the beasts from farmers – 5¢ a pound – and that's the way he sold it. So hamburger, round steak, sirloin, rib roasts were all the same price. He had a great red carcass hanging in the ice room – never more than one – which he heaved out and flopped onto his big cutting table. You pointed out which piece you wanted and he hacked it off. I don't think we've ever eaten better – meatwise – than we did as his customers.

We ate well in other ways, too, because of the system of relief and our friendship with the municipal secretary, Vincent Denis. We weren't actually on relief, being among the lucky teachers who got paid, but many of the rural teachers were. It's the only time I know of that fully-employed workers were given the pokey.

But we did come in for some of the produce that was

shipped from Eastern Canada for the relief of the starving farmers. Somehow the people of the East had come to realize that, although the depression there had practically ended by 1935, because of the terrible drought it was still going strong in Saskatchewan. So churches and other benevolent organizations got together and shipped food to us. This consisted mostly of cheddar cheese, windfall apples and salt cod.

The cheese was wonderful. I remember getting great chunks of it, old and mellow, and we ate it in every way that cheese can be eaten. The windfall apples were not bad, except by the time we'd cut away the bruised parts it took a lot of them to make a decent-sized bowl of applesauce. But the cod fish was a complete disaster.

Saskatchewan residents have never been big fish eaters and with so much protein running about on the hoof had never been introduced to the "protein of the sea." We simply didn't know what to do with it. I remember coming home with four huge slabs, holding them at arm's length because of the stink, and plunking them down on the kitchen table.

"What in the world is that?" Aileen asked, moving furtively towards the living room.

"Cod fish. Great stuff. Full of protein."

"Couldn't you have got some that hadn't gone bad?"

"It's not bad. That's the way it's supposed to smell."

Even Jonesy, the cat, and a dog we'd lately acquired named Puddles left the kitchen in disgust.

"Come on," I said. "What's everybody acting so crazy for? Cod fish is the staple diet of many people in the world. Considered a great delicacy in Newfoundland."

"What's that white stuff on it?"

I tasted it. "Salt. I guess that's so it won't spoil."

"Hah! How am I supposed to cook it?"

"The way you cook any fish, I guess. Put it in the frying pan. Bake it. Suit yourself."

"If I suited myself, I'd throw it out."

"Okay, I'll cook it."

First off, I tried to cut it up with the carving knife but I couldn't make a dent in the board-like slab. Then I tried the paring knife but that wouldn't work, either. Finally I took it outside and chopped it with the axe. One of the chunks flew off like a chip and landed in the ash pile. I brushed it off and it looked as good as the others.

Turned out that chopping it up was the easiest part. The stuff absolutely refused to fry. Just sat there in the pan and stank. I put lots of bacon fat with it, too, but it didn't help. Nothing helped. When I finally removed the stinking, blackened, beat-up but still hard mess from the pan and tried to eat it, I couldn't manage one bite. I didn't know what to do with it then. Couldn't put it in the garbage for we had no garbage pail. Finally threw it out onto the slop pile where it promptly froze. But when spring came the stink was so bad I had to bury the stuff away out in the field behind the house.

Ever since then I've had nothing to do with cod fish. If I see it in a meat counter I shy away to another part of the store. People tell me it's delicious, either smoked or fresh or even salted, if it's soaked and cooked correctly. But I'm taking no chances. Cod fish and I have absolutely no rapport. The depression did things like that to people.

I have only a couple more things to say about the little house on the edge of town. When spring came it turned out to be more of a cottage on the edge of a lake. Beside us was an immense slough that extended across our garden right up to the house. The box elders surrounding the lot were reflected in its water; frogs sang from its depth. I made a raft out of some old railway ties and boards that were lying around and pushed myself around the slough, and I got a pair of rubber boots.

As a kid in Nokomis and Prince Albert I had always

wanted a pair of rubber boots that would come up to my knees. I had a great weakness for water and as soon as the snow melted I'd start wading in it and get my feet wet. My parents tried everything they knew to prevent me from doing this – scoldings, threats, shamings – but nothing worked. They would never lick a kid for having wet feet. My parents only licked kids when they lost their tempers and couldn't help themselves. They never got mad enough about wet feet, just disgusted.

I almost got a pair of rubber boots once in Nokomis when I was five. I coaxed Dad and coaxed him until he gave in and took me down to McEwen's store to get a pair. But when I took off my shoes to try them on it was revealed that my stockings were soaking wet. Dad was even more disgusted. Said he'd be blessed – Dad was never damned, always blessed – if he'd buy rubber boots for a kid who couldn't keep his feet dry.

Anyway, when I saw this great grand body of water stretching away from the back door, I decided that at last I would have a pair of rubber boots. After all I was my own man and certainly too old to get my feet wet. So I went down to Nikoluk's store and for $1.95 got myself the finest pair of rubber boots I've ever seen. Thick red soles, they had, with a deep tread and a nice fabric lining. I brought them home and just sat looking at them – marvelling at their beauty. "Look at those soles," I said, and Aileen tried her best to be impressed. Then I put them on and waded into the slough. I wanted to see how far I could wade without the water going over the top, you see, and of course the only way I could accomplish this was to let the water go over the top.

Aileen watched the performance in disbelief. And when I'd waded back and sat on the back step and thoughtfully dumped the water out of my boots, she said, "What in the world did you do that for?" I started to explain but then I quit. Women don't understand about rubber boots.

Then there were the bees.

Away at the back of the yard was our two-holer. It really was a fine one, sturdy and strong – sturdy enough in fact to withstand being lifted over the back fence on Hallowe'en night and carried half a mile away to the fair grounds – and painted a nice green colour. It was a comforting place on an early summer morning with the birds twitting about and the grasshoppers leaping past the door. I liked to leave the door open so I could see across the fields and think.

But then one day when Aileen's sister Doris was visiting us, she came running back towards the house yelling that there was a bee after her. I investigated, of course, and discovered to my chagrin that a swarm of bees had taken up residence in a gopher hole right in front of the outhouse door. Now this was a real problem, one that dealt with the fundamentals of life. Bees at the backhouse! And it was a problem the solution of which could not be put off for long.

So I dealt with it. But you don't go mucking about with bees with impunity. After they had chased me back to the house I dressed up for the job. First a pair of long overalls which I tucked into my rubber boots. Then a heavy smock, then an old fedora with a piece of curtain tied over it and securely around my neck. A pair of gauntlet gloves completed the uniform. I was ready for the bees.

They were ready for me, too. First I tried pouring a tub of wash water down the hole, but that didn't do any good. Then I poured coal-oil down and tried to light it. I couldn't. Then I filled the boiler with water and boiled it and heaved that out and poured it down. The bees didn't care – in fact they probably liked it since it was such a dry summer. At any rate, they showed absolutely no tendency to move.

All this time the crisis was becoming more and more acute. An immediate solution *had* to be found. Suddenly I had a brilliant idea. I would *dig* the rascals out. So I got out a spade and sent Aileen to the farm behind to borrow a pickaxe from Mr. Tournier, got my digging fork and went to work. It turned out to be a blazing hot day and, dressed as I was in heavy overalls, smock, rubber boots, felt fedora and curtains, I soon began to sweat. Drought had made the ground rock-hard and the more I dug the harder I sweated.

For some reason no bees appeared at all and so in desperation I began to tear off my gear. First the hat and curtain, then the smock, then the overalls and finally the rubber boots. So there I was, naked as a jay bird except for a pair of tattered shorts, swinging that pick. As is usual, when I work hard and sweat hard, I also swear hard, which I figured didn't matter since we were on the edge of town and nobody was about.

I'd got down about two feet when my pick hit something soft and papery and a million bees poured out of that hole. I made for the house as fast as I could go, yelling for Aileen to have the door open when I got there and yanking off my shorts to rid them of bees. When I got inside Aileen and Doris had withdrawn from the kitchen to the living room from which came bursts of suppressed laughter.

"What's so bloody funny about a man being attacked by bees?" I roared at them.

Aileen peered out from the living room, her face very red and her cheeks puffed. She motioned to the window and all she said was, "Look!"

I looked and there was a whole line of beat-up pick-up trucks, waggons and Bennett buggies. They were farmers on their way into town for Saturday's shopping. And on seeing the apparition in the back yard they had naturally stopped to see what was going on. My impromptu strip-tease had been witnessed by half the farmers in the countryside. Now more than ever they were convinced that I was nuts.

That fall I became a playwright, a play producer, a play director and an actor. I was the Noel Coward of Wannego, young, brilliant, sophisticated, witty, and willing. With the confidence that comes from ignorance and youth, I was sure that I could do anything as well as anybody else. The play came off all right, but I hadn't reckoned on the kind of calamities that can follow when you begin to put words into other people's mouths.

The whole thing began with Beulah Stoneman, wife of Sergeant Stoneman of the RCMP. Beulah was a small woman, small and blonde and beautiful. She was also quiet, refined and cultured. A complete contrast to her husband.

Concerning Beulah, the women of the town would say – "She's too good for him. Such a sweet little thing. I don't know how she ever came to marry that great, insensitive brute of an Ernest." They all agreed that she was an angel and he was a thug who treated her abominably.

He did, too. Behaved towards her as though she were a trollop. Scoffed at her artistic interests (she was among other things president of the Literature and Reading Club), told dirty stories in her presence, slapped her round little posterior as she walked past his chair. She never fought back or even admonished him for his rough ways, but only smiled a small enigmatic smile and went on with what she was saying. With my superior acumen I had decided that their marriage was a grotesque sham.

Aileen and I occasionally played bridge with the Stonemans – before the founding of the Wannego Bridge Club, that is – and one evening when we arrived at their place Beulah was obviously too excited to play. She greeted us at the door, sat us down in the living room and announced,

"Do you know what I think? This town needs a dramatic society."

Ernest threw up his big hands and exploded. "Don't listen to her. This town needs a dramatic society like it needs another eight bootleggers."

"Please, dear," Beulah admonished. "Let me explain what I mean."

"I know what you mean. And you're not getting me into any damned play. That's for sure."

She smiled at him as a mother smiles at a child. "Of course not, dear. This will have nothing to do with you. It's for more . . . well . . . artistic people."

I wasn't much more enthusiastic than Ernest. A dramatic society would only mean one thing to me – more work and less time for writing.

"Uh . . . I think maybe Ernest's right," I began. "There's hardly enough talent . . . I mean. . . ."

"Talent! Why the town's crawling with talent. I studied drama at university and . . ." she played her trump . . . "we've even got a practically professional playwright right here in town!"

Beulah had taken an interest in my writing. She'd ask me all sorts of questions about it while Ernest sat there and said things like – "Well, are we going to play bridge or are we going to talk this artsy-fartsy stuff all night?" True, she never actually bothered to enquire if I sold anything or not. Such practical matters were too mundane for her thinking and I never went out of my way to explain that I was Canada's busiest unpublished writer.

So the bit about a "practically professional playwright" got to me. Why not? Here was a chance to try out my stuff on the stage. Besides, the *Writers' Digest* had just run an article about the tremendous market for material in the tent shows in the U.S. They paid for plays on a royalty basis, and some writers had made small fortunes out of writing for the market. The article outlined the type of play that was needed. A nice, homey, clean, funny play generally referred to as "comedy drama." The standard characters were the ingénue, the leading man, the villain – or villainess – the toby and so on. I'd acted in dozens of them with names like *The Little Clodhopper, The Road to the City, Just Plain Hank*, and so on. If I wrote one and tried it out here in Wannego I could get it into shape to sell to the tent shows.

The upshot of this was that we held an organizational meeting for the Wannego "Academy des Beaux Arts." Yes, I admit that was the name. Not my name, but Beulah's. "We don't want any silly little name like the Wannego Dramatic Society," she said. "This is going to be much bigger."

We couldn't advertise in the newspaper because there was no newspaper, but we tacked up a notice in the post office and had the preachers announce it in the churches and we told the kids at school to tell their parents about it. The turnout was fantastic – twenty-three women and two men. We'd run smack into the English-French thing, of course. The Smith group didn't come because they thought they might run into some of the Beltier group and the Beltier group didn't come for the same reason. That is the men didn't come. The women didn't pay much attention to the feud and mingled in a variety of organizations. The other man who came, besides myself, was none other than Archie, the Apologetic Apothecary.

I must digress a bit here to explain about Archie, the Apologetic Apothecary. We always called him that but some others in town called him "that damned queer druggist" or "the fidgety pharmacist."

His name was Archie Archenborough and he was the shyest man I've ever known. He would blush if you passed the time of day with him. He never should have gone into pharmacy; there are too many intimate connotations to the job. The ladies just loved to watch his face when they asked him for a box of sanitary pads or any other article of female equipment.

And the men, well, he was their meat. I'll swear guys like Archie are somehow sent to small towns to relieve the monotony of existence. Hodge Hopkins dropped in on Archie at least once a day. If he had nothing else to do, no kids to tease, no dogs to set against each other, he could always find some simple, innocent amusement with Archie.

It was Hodge who was largely responsible for a classic incident involving Archie, Hodge and a big constipated farmer called Tightass Wembley. Wembley was a bachelor who had a good piece of land north of town where he always seemed, even during the worst drought years, to get some crop. He was the stingiest man in the district, too stingy by miles to ever get married. He'd been engaged for five years to Maggie Delp, they said, but could never bring himself to spend the money on a wedding. Finally Maggie gave up and went away to Saskatoon where she married a real estate man and raised a bunch of kids.

So Tightass lived alone in solitary squalor. Apart from money matters, on which he was as cunning as a Wall Street broker, Tightass was as ignorant as the horses he drove. He read nothing, was too tight to buy a radio, and talked almost entirely in swear words. In this regard, though, he was something of an artist and produced the most colourful similes I ever heard in a province noted for colourful similes.

Everybody called him Tightass. It was one of those nicknames that through use has lost its crudeness. To be sure, refined ladies shortened it to Titus which was a perfectly respectable name. As a matter of fact, for a long time I thought that was his name until I heard the story of how he acquired the nickname Tightass.

It happened when Archie first came to town and he was even shyer – if that's possible – than when we knew him. It was all but impossible to get him to say anything. He'd sort of slink out from behind the display cards piled on top of his counter and stand there blushing, and staring at one of his shoes.

One day Wembley came in and he was in a bad way. "What have you got," he demanded of Archie, "that will loosen me up?"

"I uh – beg your pardon?" muttered Archie, trying not to look at this big tub of a man.

"I'm bunged up tighter's a bull's arse in fly time."

Archie blushed deeper and backed up against the toothpaste.

"I need something to make me shit!" Wembley exploded. "And I need it now!"

"What have you tried?" Archie managed to ask.

"Everything. Prunes, senna leaves, salts, castor oil. Name it and I've tried it."

Without exposing himself further to this crudeness, Archie fished in a drawer and pulled out a small box of suppositories and handed them across the counter to Tightass. The big man turned the box over, read only the print large enough for him to see, and inquired, "Rectal application? What does that mean?"

But there was no way he was going to get an explanation on that subject from Archie who had gone so red that it looked as though he was going to burst. So Tightass stuffed the box in his pocket and went out onto the street where, as bad luck would have it, he encountered Hodge Hopkins. The farmer asked the same question of Hodge and Hodge said, "Oh that doesn't mean nothing. You just eat 'em, same as any medicine."

So there and then Tightass devoured the entire box of suppositories.

Two days later he came into town and roared into the drug store. Hodge saw him go in and followed close behind. For what happened in the store we have only Hodge's word, but it sounds authentic. Tightass approached the counter, his face purple with rage. "That stuff you gave me to make me shit!" he roared. "It didn't work."

"I'm sorry . . ." Archie began, but Tightass cut him off.

"Ate the whole damned box. Nothing! For all the good they did me I might as well have shoved them up my ass!"

Where was I? Oh yes, the meeting.

We spent most of that first meeting listening to various wives describing what a bunch of uncultured slobs the men of Wannego really were and how this proved that in a little town nothing really worth while could be accomplished. But by now I was keen to get the thing going and I persuaded them that I could get some of the senior boys to come and we would surely have enough for a play. After they see what a marvelous job we make of our first production, I said, they will be falling over themselves to join the Academy. So we organized.

I got busy and wrote a rip snorter of a play. It had everything, humour, pathos, drama, suspense, fascinating characters, dramatic irony. It was set in the rotunda of a hotel, which gave us plenty of exits and entrances and a place where travelling men gather. It was called *Train to Nowhere*, I remember, and it had to do with this beautiful, innocent young school-teacher who boards at the hotel and who had fallen into the clutches of a villainous travelling man who wanted her to go to the city with him on the midnight train. To do this he was blackmailing her regarding some money that had been stolen from the till, and she thought her young boy friend had taken it and her boy friend thought she had taken it, and each was trying to protect the other. A truly original plot.

The toby in the play was my favorite. He was the night clerk, modelled right after Mickey Rooney, and he was an amateur radio operator (or ham) who was always making contact with other hams in far parts of the world. Another touch of genius, I remember, was an immense potted plant in the rotunda, which was excellent for people to hide behind and listen to conversations of others and just catch enough of it so as to get all mixed up. It was, as the playbills later proclaimed, "A fast-moving, hilarious comedy of errors that will pull at your heart-strings while itching your funny-bone."

Casting it was something of a problem. There was only one person for the beautiful, demure school-teacher and that of course was Beulah Stoneman. Opposite her we had to put our one male, Archie, and I wrote the part to suit him – very shy and awkward, but coming on strong at the end. I didn't know quite how I was going to manage that, but I'd have to try. For the toby we got Sammy Holden, one of my senior students who was also a pain in the neck. He was lively, funny, full of silly questions, and puns, imaginative and energetic. Just the kind of student teachers hate. I thought that by putting him in the play I could help him use up his excess energy. The female hotel owner was easy to cast, as were the gossiping matrons who gathered there to tear the heroine apart. I had to play the villain part myself, which I did in a Mephistophelian beard. We were all ready to go.

We had our first practice in our living room, during which we just read through the play. And I discovered a most horrible truth. My lines were terrible. Speeches that sounded so lively and scintillating to me as I wrote them came out trite, dull and ridiculous. Not because the players were inept – that too – but because the lines were very bad. They needed a lot of work.

There were other problems. To spare anybody too much embarrassment, I had cut the love scenes down to a minimum – little more than holding hands and a slight peck on the cheek. That would never do, Beulah protested, these people were supposed to be in love, passionately in love. They'd have to show it. So it was back to the drawing-board to re-write the play.

The next read through was better. The speeches were shorter and snappier and more to the point. In fact there were some pretty good comedy lines.

So we were ready for the first reading on the stage.

Now I discovered another disquieting fact. Writing for the stage is precise and exact in the extreme. You can't, for instance, have a character say something after you've had him "exit left." Also there is no point in having one character whisper to another when they are at opposite sides of the stage. Whispers don't do well, anyway, on the stage since nobody can hear them. So it was back to the drawing-board again.

This time I made a model of the stage about three feet wide. Put in little blocks of wood to represent the furniture and used little toy soldiers for my characters. At least I managed not to have them running into each other and to keep their exits and entrances straight.

Finally I had people moving about as they should, and saying lines that didn't sound like ridiculous rot. Now to get the cast to sound just a little bit like real people.

I'll not be so pretentious as to attempt a dissertation on how to direct a play, a subject about which I knew practically nothing. But then, as I've said, knowing nothing about a subject or a task never stopped me from trying it. Speak so that you can be heard at the back, I told them, face the audience as much as possible, and don't stand in front of the person who is speaking. Oh yes, learn your lines, pick up your cues and be sure to exit and enter at the right time and place. That was all I knew about play directing, and that was what I told them.

Directing amateur theatricals is tricky at best. In the first place, the players know nothing about the acting craft, but think they know everything. In the second place, since they are not being paid, they miss practices, come late, come drunk, fool around during rehearsals and quit if you are mean to them. Worst of all, they display all sorts of quirks to their personality that you never dreamed of in everyday contact with them. In short, they become temperamental.

I suppose all this is because they have legitimately entered the world of fantasy. All their day-dreaming and fanciful ideas about themselves can now be expressed in the character they are playing. Thus it was that Archie became a different person as soon as he got on the stage. He shed his shyness as a snake sheds its old skin. He became aggressive, forthright and charming, reminding me somewhat of Cary Grant in his prime. But most of all, as practices progressed, it became obvious that he was falling in love with Beulah.

Beulah Stoneman responded to this in a remarkable way. She obviously enjoyed being treated as some sort of goddess. Her big blue eyes would light up when Archie came near her, which he did at every opportunity, and when she took his hand or touched him it was in a manner that every man dreams of being touched. I'd never seen her act that way with Ernest, or anything approaching it. What an actress! I gloated. This play is really going to be something.

Their love scenes on stage were a director's dream. What had at first been tentative gropings became long, passionate embraces. Often while waiting for me to finish some direction to another member of the cast they would stand, hand in hand, gazing into each other's eyes as only lovers gaze, and when they were off-stage in the dark alleys and cubbyholes at the back and sides they were always together, doing heaven knows what.

Ernest never came to rehearsals, of course, much preferring when not on duty to play smear with the boys. Besides, since the Wannego detachment had two other towns in its care and all of the surrounding country, he was out of town a good deal. He was too preoccupied to notice any change in his wife's behavior.

Aileen noticed it though. She had a variety of jobs in the production – prompter, assistant director and assistant writer among others – and she couldn't help but be aware of what was happening on and off the stage.

"What are you going to do about it?" she asked.

"About what?"

"You mean you haven't been watching those two love birds? Everybody else has."

"They're just throwing themselves into their parts."

"They're throwing themselves into a lot of trouble."

"Oh come now."

"Are you aware that the rest of the cast are making bets on what will happen when Ernest sees this production?"

"What's the betting?"

"About even money for Ernest shooting them both from his seat or stomping on stage and breaking Archie's back."

"Hmmm . . . the play's ending always has bothered me. Now if that were to happen . . . Yes . . ."

"Joke if you want to, but I tell you there's going to be some fur flying if you can't calm those two down. And some of that fur might be yours."

I must admit that up until then I'd been viewing this situation with sardonic pleasure. Poetic justice or some such notion is what I had in mind. But this put an entirely different light on the thing. Ernest did have a frightful temper, as everybody knew, and he was quite capable of breaking the director-writer-producer's back along with that of his main target.

"Maybe there'll be a murder up north or something that night and he won't see the play."

"*That night*? This play is running for *three* nights, remember, and already Beulah is talking of taking it to at least three other towns. She's going to make a career of it."

"Yeah, and Ernest is well known in all of those towns, and not too popular with large segments of the population.

Maybe I should speak to Archie . . . get him to tone it down a little . . . you know . . ."

"Lots of luck. That man is in love. It shines from his eyes. His is the irresistible force."

As the date of the production drew closer the town and district took more and more interest in the proceedings. The women in charge of publicity got their posters printed . . . by hand . . . and distributed to the merchants along the main street. Hilda Mawhinney who was something of an artist had done an illustration that looked like Anita Ekberg and Orson Bean in passionate embrace. And when the members began to sell tickets they were in for a surprise.

"Imagine!" Yvonne Beltier, in charge of ticket sales exclaimed. "Everybody seems to want them. I thought we'd have a terrible time selling fifty and we've sold over a hundred already. The Ukrainians north of town are buying them like mad. Joe Perverseff alone bought ten reserved seats in the eighth row centre. He must be bringing his entire family."

Joe Perverseff, I remembered, was the man whose daughter's wedding Ernest had interrupted in such a dramatic manner. He was a man whom I never suspected of being interested in the theatre, especially the English-speaking theatre. But I knew why he was coming, all right, and so did everybody else in the district.

It was a strange situation, really; everybody knew what was going on except Ernest. And nobody was going to tell him for fear of getting his head knocked off. Even the other Mounties of the detachment, three younger single men who boarded at the hotel, finally heard rumours of it. But they, too, weren't about to tell their boss. I felt like a man on a toboggan sliding down an icy slope who knows he's heading for a fence at the bottom but can't stop.

Besides my play was my real worry. Everything was going wrong. The town carpenter, who had little else to do, had agreed to make the sets for us, but just at the last he'd been hired to build a chicken coop and of course couldn't afford to put that off. So he was behind. The prop man hadn't been able to find a potted plant and Mrs. Polonski at the hotel, not being too sure she liked having her rotunda represented on the stage, was loath to loan hers. The costume mistress was behind with the costumes and nobody really knew their lines. Except for those love scenes between Beulah and Archie the play was a mess.

The dress rehearsal was a shambles, again except for Beulah and Archie, and the next night, Thursday, was opening night. After school I'd gone down to the post office to see what manuscripts along with rejection slips had returned and in front of the hardware store I met Ernest. God, he was a big man in uniform: polished boots, polished buttons, big round hat, tunic with Sam Browne belt – and gun!

We passed the time of day.

"Well," I said tentatively, "tonight's the night."

"What night?" He seemed jumpy.

"The play. I . . . uh . . . don't suppose you'll be going."

"Yeah, I'll be going. Wife's made me promise."

"She has?"

"Yeah, insists on it. Never seen her so insistent about anything. But I don't like the look of it . . . the feel of it . . ."

"The feel of what?"

"This town. Something's brewing, I can smell it. These damned Ukes . . . you never know with them. There's a kind of restlessness around . . . like just before that big fight on the street two years ago. If I was smart I'd get out of town."

"Why don't you?"

"Wife would kill me. She says I'll be real proud of her." Then he laughed his hearty laugh.

But, as it turned out, he didn't get to see the play that first night. Some guy in a new Ford V-8 went roaring down the highway at eighty-five miles an hour and Ernest gave chase. He caught him about twenty miles from town and by the time he'd brought him back and charged him and lodged him in the jail until he could prove he hadn't stolen the car – which he couldn't – the cast were taking their curtain calls.

The play? Well, as a comedy it was a complete flop. I learned something then that I was to realize many times again when I got around to writing radio comedy for Buckingham Theatre and Ford Theatre: you can't have a comedy without a comedian. The lines you think are excruciatingly funny when you mentally hear them coming from the mouth of Billy de Wolf, for instance, just sound foolish coming from the mouth of Sammy Holden, or anybody else with no sense of comedy timing.

As a melodrama it was fair. It followed all the rules, built to a nice climax and the good people triumphed and the villain failed, just as they always do in melodrama. It moved along fast enough, and I believe most of the kids in the audience and even some of the adults were actually concerned about how it would turn out.

But as a love story it was superb. Beulah and Archie were so convincing that even those who had come to sneer and laugh were moved. I had ambivalent feelings about this. Like Svengali I had created a person. Archie was no longer shy and awkward and self-effacing. He was a lion, filled with self-confidence and persuasion. Never again, I told myself, would he be the butt of the village jokes. Never again would anyone be able to tease him in the curling rink or the beer parlour. He had become a man.

The second night the play went better: fewer missed cues, muffed lines and props that weren't where they should be. The cast had lost its initial nervousness, and Sammy even managed to get a few laughs where he should get them. Once again Sergeant Stoneman's duties had kept him away and I found myself forgetting about him completely.

Came the final night. The first thing I saw when, ensconced in my Mephistophelian beard, I peeked out through the curtain was Sergeant Stoneman. There he sat, bulking huge and awesome in the third row, centre. Certainly he'd be able to see and hear everything that happened on stage. What would he do? He was capable, I knew, of climbing up and punching Archie in the mouth and toting his struggling wife off with him. For one panicky moment I thought of stepping out onto the apron and announcing that due to a mysterious virus that had laid low the entire cast there would be no performance tonight. But I didn't, and before I knew it the curtain was going up.

The play opened with Sammy on stage fooling with his ham radio set. His call letters were "Ten-Q," I remember, which were good for punning, and there was a lot more of the same. That gives you some idea of the kind of play it was. During the course of contacting somebody in Aklavik and getting all mixed with solar pears and sarp heals and lorthern nights – spoonerisms were his stock in trade – he managed to tell the audience where the play was set and something about the characters. A damned clever device.

Then Bernadette came on, to a nice little round of applause, and told him her problem. The rich industrialist – in the Thirties all villains were industrialists – from the city wanted to marry her and give her everything she could ever want.

"Then why don't you marry him?" asked Toby.

"Because I don't love him."

"Gosh, I'd marry him in a minute. Do you suppose if I put on a wig and . . ." This will give you some more idea.

Then Bernadette made a nice little speech about true love being important and in came Harold, the honest but true bank clerk who was studying nights to better himself and was altogether a most admirable chap. It was obvious to everyone that he loved Bernadette and she loved him but that he was too poor to ever ask her to marry him.

Beulah, I Love You

Thus the conflicts had been neatly established and we were away. I wasn't very good that night. It's hard to keep your mind on the stage and your eye on a Sergeant in the darkened house and try to gauge his reactions. Being the smooth persuader, I was the first one to take Bernadette in my arms and kiss her, a part I'd rather enjoyed up until that night, but now I gave her a slight brush on the cheek and got roundly booed from the audience for it.

I thought that I'd maybe set the tone for Beulah and Archie. Maybe they'd cool the love scenes, too. But they didn't. If anything, they were more torrid than ever and when the part came for Bernadette to weep and tell her love that she must marry another, I could see real tears on her cheeks.

Strange things had happened on that stage, but they weren't half as strange as what happened after the curtain went up for the national anthem. Everybody in the opera house from ancient farmer to toddler sensed that the real drama was yet to come. After some small, polite applause a hush fell over the room. Even a baby who had begun to whimper shut up. Everyone was looking at Ernest Stoneman.

What would he do? No man likes to be made a fool of. Less so in public. Least of all by the man who is the butt of village jokes.

Nothing in Ernest's face revealed how he felt. He got up and pushed back his chair and moved out into the aisle. People drew back as he passed. I can still see him striding down that aisle towards the stage, all six-foot-four of him. I'll swear he got taller and wider as he approached.

On the stage the usual fuss and flutter was going on with the actors hugging each other, and saying how great they'd been. Especially Beulah and Archie who were still in a semi-stunned state from their triumph. They stood in the centre of the stage with the others crowding around.

Then one by one everyone noticed Ernest. He clumped

up the steps at the right of the stage, parted the side curtain and stood looking at the scene. As they became aware of his presence members of the cast fell silent and drew back from the two at centre stage. Archie came back to reality with a shudder. Good gracious, he must have asked himself, what am I doing here holding onto the hand of the Sergeant's wife! But he didn't let go. He straightened up to his full five-foot-ten and faced his adversary.

A couple of possibilities flashed through my mind. Like shouting "Fire!" and heading for the nearest exit. Or at least going to the middle of the stage and getting between Ernest and his prey. But like the others I couldn't move. I stared fascinated as at the Frankenstein monster stalking a child.

Ernest had one hand in his tunic pocket, the other was loose at his side. As he came up to his wife and her stage lover he raised his right hand and we all cringed a little. But when it came down, it came down gently on the top of Archie's head in a friendly pat. "You did real well, Sonny," he said. "You really did."

Then he pulled his other hand out of the pocket and held it out to his wife. Dangling from the big fingers was a pearl necklace.

I realized something about Ernest Stoneman then that I should have known all along. Rough he certainly was and crude, too, but not stupid. He had done exactly the right thing. Since there was no jeweller in town he had obviously driven to Saskatoon to get the pearls. Ernest – who nobody thought would go across the street for anyone! It was a magnificent gesture – and it worked. That necklace pulled little Beulah right out of the never-never land of play acting and into Ernest's big arms. All the make-believe passion she'd thought she had for her stage lover became the real thing for her real man.

"Come on," Ernest said, lifting her in his arms. "Let's get the hell out of here."

Beulah, I Love You

Beulah never again mentioned taking the show on the road.

Archie? He reverted to his old shy self. And the boys went right on kidding him at the curling rink, but never about the play.

The play? After its great success in Wannego I was sure it would be a hit with the producers of the tent shows. I re-worked it, sharpened the lines even more, dreaming all the while of years of royalties to be reaped from its success. Then Aileen re-typed it beautifully and we put the clean pages into an envelope and sent it off to one of the agents listed in the *Writers' Digest* article. In due course I received a postcard with some barely readable printing on it which said the manuscript had been received and would be made available to producers. I never heard another word, nor received a cent in royalties.

But the play had helped me. Thinking of it out there in the world of drama, being read, possibly, by producers gave me that tiny dribble of hope without which I never could have continued. For there is, I'm convinced, a limit to the number of times you can lower the pail into the well and have it come up empty. Sooner or later you decide the well of hope is indeed dry and you might better try something else.

I have never had much enthusiasm for the royal and ancient game of curling. When the craze for the game hit the East and every golf club became a curling rink and the game became an absolute social must in town and city alike, I still held off. When asked why I'd mumble something about not being very good at games or being too busy or having a bad back. How could I explain that my enthusiasm for the game had been completely killed by one horrible, ghastly, miserable, traumatic all-night bonspiel.

Curling has been the main winter pastime in Saskatchewan for as long as there's been a Saskatchewan, I guess, and before that. One of my earliest memories is of being left with my brothers and sisters in the big stone house in Nokomis while Mother and Dad were over at the rink curling. And of the great prizes Dad and my brothers would bring home – chairs, couches, fancy lamps, garden sets, and so on.

It was the perfect game for the prairies, for it is played on ice and ice is what Saskatchewan always had plenty of. Besides, we had none of the modern winter blessings in those days. No television, no radio, no moving pictures. Just house-parties with dancing and singing, and curling.

It was much the same in the Thirties, more so perhaps because money was so scarce. Curling cost little at that time. The annual curling club fee rarely ran more than five dollars and the rocks were provided. You had to buy a broom, to be sure, and that set you back almost a dollar. For the rest, the farmers just dressed as they did for work. Oh, here and there you'd see a white jumbo-knit sweater but they were considered pure swank rather than something to strive for.

I managed to avoid curling the first winter we were in Wannego, but the second winter I wasn't so lucky. Harry King came up to me one day in November and said, "I suppose you are going to curl this year."

"Well, I hadn't thought of it."

"I think we should enter a rink from the school."

"Why?"

"Well, we've never done it. Teachers just curl with somebody else. Time we showed them we can come up with just as good a rink as anybody."

My obvious remark here would be another "Why?," but I suddenly caught on. Harry wanted to be a skip and his chances didn't look good. But if we entered a rink from the school, well, being the boss he'd naturally be the skip.

The other obvious thing to say would be that I'd never curled before, but I couldn't do that. To admit that you hadn't curled would be like admitting that you'd never shot a gun or cast a fishing line or done any of those other things which make a man truly a MAN.

So I just said that I wasn't really very good at the game and that I was – uh – rather busy.

Harry didn't even listen to that. "I've entered the rink," he said. "You will be Lead, Larry Petrie will be Second. Looie Third, and I guess I'll have to Skip."

"Looie – the bootlegger? He curls?"

"Of course. Everybody curls. Looie's a great guy to take along on all-night bonspiels."

This was the first I'd heard about all-night bonspiels and later I discovered that saying that about Looie is like saying Bobby Orr is a fairly handy man to have on a hockey team.

So, along with all my other community chores, which incidentally included organizing bonspiels for the school kids to be played on outdoor sheets of ice with jam pails full of frozen sand for rocks, I became a curler.

The first night I went to the curling rink was a revelation. It was a long, low, ramshackle building with a sagging roof, no windows and a tiny door at one end. When I entered that little door I was in a room about twenty-five feet wide and ten feet deep that was packed almost solid with men. The air was foul with cigar, cigaret and pipe smoke, and the smell of farmers who wore the same overshoes here that they wore in the barn. Everybody was talking and laughing and in great spirits. I was glad I'd come.

The inside wall of this room was all windows through which could be seen the two sheets of curling ice, smooth and gleaming and brilliantly lit. On benches in front of these windows sat the real experts of the game, watching and assessing every shot that was made and endlessly going over the past performances of each curler.

"I think he's a bit light."

"No . . . no . . . he's coming in nice there . . . see . . ."

"He's going to just nudge it . . . Ah . . . went right past. Tom's been missing a lot of them kind lately."

"Yeah. I mind when he'd make a shot like that with his eyes closed. 'Member the spiel of '32 when he and Dad Trainor were tied coming home and Tom made that inside draw? As fine a piece of curling as I've ever seen."

And on and on and on.

As for the rest of the men in the room, they were visiting. Bringing each other up to date on the condition of their livestock and families. Telling dirty stories. Hodge Hopkins always had the latest story from the city, picked up from a travelling salesman. I don't know what it's like now, but in those days a travelling salesman might just as well not bother coming into a town if he didn't have at least a couple of new stories to tell. Each story would be greeted by a great explosion of laughter.

Every so often the door would burst open to let in a blast of frigid air, a billow of freezing mist, and a new comer who made directly for the big iron stove that stood in the middle of the room. "Man . . . it's cold enough to freeze the balls off a brass monkey. Where's the draw?"

Then he'd go over to the blackboard where Harry King, secretary of the club, had neatly printed the names of the teams and the draws.

Every night during the winter this went on. On Thursday night the rink was taken over by the women curlers. Now and then there was some mixed curling, but nobody took it very seriously. Curling was one place where men and women just shouldn't mix.

Having never curled before, I watched the game closely that first night and listened to the comments of the curlers. I knew the rules of the game, having watched my father and brothers at it a few times, but I had to learn exactly how it was done.

Finally our turn came and the four of us went out onto the ice. I tried out my new broom as I'd seen others do (I'd been practising sweeping on the kitchen floor all week), and was assigned to a pair of rocks. As Lead I'd have to throw those damned rocks first and I knew that everybody in the waiting room would be watching to see how "that teacher" was going to do. And I knew, too, that this first rock was the crucial one. From it they would enter me into the computers of their minds as "good," "fair," "poor," or "not worth a damn."

It might be argued that I should have shot for the last category and ended my curling career right there. But that wouldn't work. I had to live with these people, had to maintain some sort of status so as not to become another Archie Archenborough. If that happened my position in Wannego would be untenable. The disdain would soon filter down to the kids in school and my discipline would be ruined. No, in order to continue on in this town I and everybody else knew that, just as sure as we knew that ice was cold and slippery.

So, I crouched there in the hack, alone in a cold world. At the other end Harry King had placed his broom a foot or so to the right of the button and was holding his left arm out stiff. This, I knew, meant the "In" turn. I aimed for the broom and slid the rock out towards it, giving it a slight twist at the last second. But I knew as soon as I let go that I'd slid the damned thing too hard. I'd be lucky if it didn't go through the end of the building. Larry and Looie, who'd taken up their positions half way down the ice, didn't make a move to sweep the speeding rock. Hell, they couldn't have caught it. I was dead.

And then I got lucky. Because this was the first rock thrown in this game and because my teammates weren't sweeping, there was something on that shiny surface just over the hog line . . . a straw maybe, or a piece of dirt. Anyway my rock caught it, slowed down and, dragging its foreign matter with it, slid up toward the tip of Harry's broom and stopped.

So there it was. I hadn't made a good shot, but then I hadn't made a bad one, either. The rock was there, a foot from the button. That was a fact that couldn't be denied. It was impossible to categorize me on that shot; there was no place in the computer for it. The wise men shook their heads and waited to see what the lead on the other rink would do with that rock of mine. I was in the game.

The lead on the other team missed the rock and it was my turn to throw again. This time I wouldn't be heavy. I wasn't. In fact the rock barely made it over the hog line. But that was all right, too, because it could be considered a guard for the first one. From the corner of my eye I saw the rail birds shaking their heads and rubbing their chins. They hadn't quite got me figured.

Curling could have been good fun, I think, if I hadn't begrudged every minute that took me away from my typewriter. I wrote a short story about curling and sent it to *Maclean's* and got it back. There was no point, I realized, sending it to an American magazine because they didn't know a curling stone from a gall-stone.

We were always having bonspiels and everybody won something. If you lost in the first round, known as the Macdonald Brier, you went down with the other losers into the Consolation Spiel, and if you lost there to the Duffers Spiel and so on down, so that everybody was in some sort of competition.

We were doing all right in the Consolation Spiel, I remember. Won our first game and then the second one which brought us into the finals against a rink skipped by Dad Trainor – and complications. If we won we would each get a Hudson Bay blanket. The second prize was the largest jar of coffee I have ever seen. It must have held a gallon.

I became very keen then. I desperately wanted one of those huge, woolly blankets. For when we went to bed at night we had to let the fire go out because we couldn't afford the coal to keep it going. So the temperature in the bedroom would sink lower and lower until we could see our breath. Aileen made us each an enormous flannelette nightgown. I can see it yet, a yard wide and right down to the floor. She would hang them out on the clothes line one at a time because she didn't want the neighbours to know her husband wore a nightie.

We'd sometimes lie in bed trying to devise means of keeping warm. I remember we figured out how a bag could be lined with feathers and closed on three sides. Then, we planned, we could crawl inside and zipper the top shut. That would keep us warm on the coldest night, we thought. Aileen made one for Beryl, but we couldn't afford the materials for one big enough for us. (Despite the poverty and deprivation of the Thirties, the birthrate in Saskatchewan held up rather well and I always considered it was due to those cold nights.)

So when we saw those snuggly blankets with their wild Indian designs on them displayed in the window of Smith's store we saw the possibility of ending our frigid nights.

Unfortunately, Harry King had quite different ideas. He'd won a Hudson Bay blanket the year before and really didn't need another because his house had a furnace in it. But he wanted that coffee. From his wife he'd learned to drink coffee as the Italians drink it, which is practically all the time, strong as lye and black as coal. Julia had a plan for the big square jar, too, which she confided to Aileen. "It's the best thing in the world for doing up dill pickles. I hope they don't win the blankets."

Our opponent in the final draw, Dad Trainor, was eighty-three years old. But he was one of those individuals that never seem to age. His skin was clear, his eyes keen, and his energy boundless. During a late-night smear session he was always the last man to suggest going home. He was up early in the morning and out on the street to see if anything was doing. Never missed a hockey game or a baseball game and was one of the best curlers in the district. The stories of his prowess on the rink were numerous and colourful, going back as far as anybody could remember. I'm quite sure that if I went back to Wannego today, thirty-five years later, I'd find Dad Trainor still sliding rocks down the shining surface of the curling rink, and laughing his big, broad-mouthed laugh.

Harry King and Dad were great pals. They didn't talk much about it but each was the other's type of man. Both were fiercely independent and individualistic. Both loved all the good things such as drink and food and sex (more than once I'd seen Dad – a widower of long standing – sneaking out the back door of the livery barn after a visit with Ruby). Both hated the fussy women of the town and especially Mrs. Shirley.

Mrs. Shirley was the nicest, kindest, the most generous of women, and the biggest pain in the neck from the Touchwood Hills to the Rockies. She had this thing about Christmas which compelled her to give everybody in town a present – and their children and their childrens' children. I remember our first Christmas when we had scraped together enough money for presents for each other and our parents. Just before the holiday Mrs. Shirley showed up with presents for both of us. Ruined the Christmas.

She ruined everybody's Christmas. Her husband, who was the station agent, had one of the preferred jobs of the Thirties and so she had more money than almost anybody else in town. Just as soon as each Christmas was over, Mrs. Shirley began making plans for the next one. Making plans and making gifts. And she talked about it and exclaimed how she'd found just the perfect thing for Mrs. Pritchard or the Harder boy. Come to think of it, she went a long way towards ruining the entire year.

A little skit that took place between King and Dad Trainor just before Christmas will illustrate Harry's feeling about all this. It happened in Smith's store, which was decorated with red and green paper and tinsel. Mrs. Shirley was picking out a last-minute present for an acquaintance and talking about it in a loud voice. Harry and Dad happened to meet close beside her and the dialogue – also in a loud voice – went something like this:

"Hello, Dad"

"Oh . . . hello, Harry. Didn't see you at first."

"Cold enough for you?"

"Cold as a frog in a frozen pool, cold as the end of an . . . well, you know."

"Yeah. Well, Merry Christmas."

"Same to you. So long. Oh . . . wait."

"What is it, Dad?"

"I completely forgot to give you your Christmas present. Here." He fished through the layers of clothing, came up with a ten-dollar bill, and ceremoniously handed it to Harry. Harry took it, put it in his pocket, shook Dad's outstretched hand and started away. He'd gone about three steps towards the door when he stopped and called to his friend:

The Night We Stole The Mountie's Car

"Oh . . . Dad . . . just a minute."

"What is it, Harry?"

"I might as well give you your present now, too." He fished into his pocket, pulled out the same ten-dollar bill and handed it to Dad without batting an eye. Again they wished each other Merry Christmas, shook hands and parted.

Everyone in the store heard and understood perfectly. After that both Harry and Dad were scratched from Mrs. Shirley's shopping list.

So we were drawn against Dad's rink in the finals. I curled as I never curled before or since. With each rock I threw I could feel the warmth of that woollen blanket embracing me. And I was good. So good in fact that I won myself a place on a rink that was going to Birchley a week later for an all-night bonspiel – and I wish I hadn't.

The whole rink curled well, with the result that we had a nice comfortable lead of two points when we were coming home. All we had to do was take out all their rocks with all our rocks and let them have the last rock and we would win by one point. But something crazy happened. Harry King, instead of playing it safe, began to call some very intricate shots – fancy draws and freezes and the like – with the result that when it came time for his last rock Dad was laying three in the house. But two of them were close together so that if Harry came down hard and hit squarely between them he'd knock both rocks out and stay in himself. We would win.

It was a shot that he could have made any day in the week. In fact, I could have made it. But this time he missed by two feet and his rock went sliding through the house. Dad's rink won the draw and the blankets. We got the coffee.

This was one of the times I was mad enough to talk back to Harry. "How in hell did you ever come to miss that shot?"

He winked at me. "I sort of lost my balance at the last minute."

"In a pig's ass you did."

"Well . . . this is probably Dad's last year of curling, you know. He's getting pretty old for the game. Kind of nice for him to win this one."

I was just about to explode into a tirade about hypocrisy and rationalization and sneakiness when I suddenly realized that he meant it. The human being's ability to lie convincingly to himself passes belief.

The following weekend was the all-night bonspiel in Birchley.

"What do you do at an all-night bonspiel?" Aileen asked.

"Curl."

"What else?"

"I don't know. I've never been on one. Sit around and watch the others curl, I guess."

"That should be fun. I hear the hotel is right next to the curling rink in Birchley. I suppose there'll be a lot of drinking."

"I suppose so. Men usually drink on occasions like this."

"What else do they do?"

"Oh . . . I get it. Well, I hear they're running a special train down with fifty houris and concubines and incense and . . . oh boy . . ."

She wasn't really being bitchy. Every wife must have a feeling of anxiety when her husband goes off on a stag do. I assured her that curling and drinking would be the extent of it. And I believed it, too.

We drove to Birchley in a caboose, a covered sleigh which, I guess was the Thirties version of the camping trailer. It consisted of a small plywood cabin built on runners. There was a little door on one side, a small window in the front so that the driver could see where he was going and through which the lines for the team extended, benches to sit on and, best of all, a little round coal-burning stove with a pipe out through the roof. A small fire in the stove kept the cabin warm, which was a good thing considering that it was thirty below outside. There were four such rigs left for Birchley that night.

This wasn't our regular rink. Besides Harry King and me, our sleigh held Hodge Hopkins and Tom Hannis, who was the Watkins man for the area and owned the sleigh. When I got to the livery barn the other guys were already there and impatient to be off. "Come on, Teacher," Hodge yelled. "Get the lead out of your ass. This is our night to howl." And then to Harry, who as usual displayed neither excitement nor animation, " Do you think this youngster is up to a night in Birchley?"

"Well, we'll just have to find out," Harry said.

We got into the sleigh where it was warm and cozy and Tom turned his team down the winding trail that went across the fields to the next town. Regular roads were snowed in during the winter months and the farmers and other travellers simply made new and more direct trails over the stubble fields. Once the team got pointed in the right direction along that trail, they needed little guidance until they'd covered the ten miles to Birchley.

As soon as we were under way Hodge Hopkins produced a crock of rye whiskey which he passed around and began to tell stories. "Did you hear the one about the constipated owl?" "No." "He couldn't shit." Then he would throw back his head and laugh loud and happily. He was feeling good. All the stupid worries about drought and relief and unpaid debts were gone. For this night at least he would think of none of them.

The journey took well over an hour and there was a good feeling in that cabin. A feeling like kids let out of school or like colts let out of the barn in spring. There was something more. A suppressed excitement that filled the sleigh but couldn't be entirely explained by the fun of curling. Little hints and leers and innuendoes popped up now and then, followed by sly laughter. I felt there was something about this trip I didn't know and should but, when I obliquely inquired, I was put off with more laughter and leers.

When we arrived I discovered that the rink was indeed next to the hotel and that the local bootlegger had a room in the hotel. All night long, curlers hurried along the board sidewalk which creaked in the cold as their weight passed along it. The rink itself was full of good fellowship and the fumes of rye whiskey. Curlers relaxed their usual stern and studious moods and tripped gaily along the ice surface, kidding each other and marvellously avoiding tripping over rocks.

It was really a full two-week holiday crammed into one night. As I began to relax with the booze and good feeling I realized how much stress I'd been under with softball games and plays and writing and teaching. I became witty, urbane, jovial. Through the fog over the ice surface and fog in my brain I saw the world as a wondrous, if slightly tilted, place. In short, I was potted.

Around about four o'clock in the morning when I was sitting in "the room" nursing a bottle of beer, Hodge Hopkins came in and said, "Hey, you haven't been to the well of ecstasy yet."

"Huh?" was my scintillating reply.

"The well of ecstasy. You haven't been."

"What in hell is the well . . ."

"Come with me."

He took me by the hand like a father taking a child, led me out of "the room" and down the dimly lighted, narrow hall to the door of another room. He knocked tentatively and a bored voice from within said, "It's okay."

Hodge started to push me through the door and then paused. "You got two bucks?"

"Well, uh, not exactly . . ."

"Here!" He thrust a two-dollar bill into my hand, urged me through the door and closed it. At first I couldn't see anything. It was an ordinary hotel bedroom with a big old bed and a wash stand with a huge porcelain pitcher on it. In the dim light from a small overhead bulb I saw there was somebody lying on the bed and that she was naked, eating chocolates from a large box on the bed beside her, and reading – of all things – *True Story Magazine*.

"Ruby!"

She peered at me in some alarm. "Who are you? Oh . . . it's the teacher!" She reached down and pulled a sheet up over her ample form. "What are you doing here?"

"What are you doing here?" I countered. It was obviously a stupid question. "What I mean is . . . how did you get here?"

"Looie brought me. He always does."

"Why that's . . . that's terrible."

"Why? The men want to have a little fun. Do you?"

Ruby was nothing if not direct. No coy flirting about her.

I felt sad and a little sick.

Despite all the plays, movies and books that show prostitution to be a gay, happy life of pleasure, I didn't think of it that way then, nor do I now. Besides, I had a wife at home and she trusted me.

But I didn't know what to do. Intellectual conversation was out. I didn't feel like preaching at the girl. She was doing her thing in the only way she could, just as the happy curlers were doing theirs. For a start I handed Ruby Hodge Hopkin's two-dollar bill.

She took it and carefully placed it with a pile of others and sort of eased herself over in the bed. I sat down on a chair beside the bed.

"Well don't take all night," she warned. "That two dollars doesn't entitle you."

"The two dollars . . ." I asked, "how much does Looie get of that? Half?"

"No, a dollar and a half."

"And you get fifty cents?"

"That's right."

"Well, how does he know . . . how many . . . I mean . . ."

"He keeps track of everybody who comes in, I don't know how he does, but he does. Hey . . . why are you asking me all these questions? Looie'll kill me if I get him in any trouble." She was frightened.

"I won't get you into any trouble." I wanted to find out more about Ruby. How had she got started as the town whore? What a great source of material she could be for a writer. "Ruby," I said, "I don't want to be with you tonight. I don't feel very well, actually, what with all the booze and all."

She brightened. "That's all right. Half the guys that come in here don't. Funny. They all ask me not to tell that they haven't. Of course I don't. A girl like me never tells nothing. That's the first thing Looie taught me."

"Was it Looie who . . . well . . . got you started? I mean was he the first one who ever . . ."

She laughed . . . a simple, ordinary laugh, not cynical, not bitter, just amused. "No, it was my father when I was about twelve, I guess."

"Your father, your own father?"

"Yes, you see my mother was sick then. My father was always good to me . . . really he was . . . and well, after all, he's my own father." She was looking at me for reassurance and I hadn't the heart to tell her that, no, not all fathers slept with their twelve-year-old daughters.

And now I felt really sick. Sick of that dingy room, sick of poverty, sick of the depression, sick of rot-gut whiskey, sick of myself, sick of that pitiful girl lying on the bed, and the rotten conditions that put her there. After all, there must be a better way to treat the mentally retarded. But most of all sick of the lousy, stinking, rotten, hypocritical society of that year-of-our-Lord 1936. It was such a sick society really, no wonder it had degenerated into the malaise of the depression and then into the cancer of the war.

I don't remember much more about that night, except that all the fun had gone and it seemed endless. We continued to curl and drink. I remember stepping on a sliding rock and falling on my backside on the ice and getting into a snarling argument with an opposing player about the penalty for such a crime. I don't remember who won. Probably nobody. Nobody was supposed to win. The curling was just an excuse for the drinking and story-telling and hanky-panky.

The trip home was a killer. All the stories had been told; all the laughter gone from us. I tried to sleep sitting up on the hard bench of the sleigh, but it didn't work. A tired voice began, "Oh he floats through the air with the greatest of ease . . ." Another joined in but soon both voices dwindled to sleepy monotones. Through the tiny window I could see a glow in the southeast and realized it must be late. It was, in fact, almost nine o'clock when we finally got back.

Since the school bell would ring at nine, I had time for nothing but a cup of coffee.

"Did you have fun?" Aileen asked.

I looked at her, so young and slim and beautiful in her nightgown. "I'd sure like to stay here with you," I said.

"Surely you're not going to school!"

"Got to. Harry King will be there. I bet he'll even be shaved. It's a matter of pride . . . or something . . . I've got to be there, too."

So I staggered off to school and sat at my desk as the kids filed into the room, grinning and looking out of the corner of their eyes at each other. They took their seats and looked up at me, fresh-faced and expectant. I dragged myself out of the chair and stood before them.

"Our civics lesson for this morning," I muttered groggily, "is equal opportunity and justice for all in a democratic society."

There are two kinds of stories, Jack Woodford said: honest sex and masked sex. Write either one. In his book *Trial and Error*, described by *Esquire* editor Arnold Gingrich as "the best damned book ever written about writing," Woodford warned against mixing the two. That way you'd offend one group of readers or the other and completely satisfy neither. He never even considered writing about anything else but sex.

Besides talking a lot of good sense about how to write stories, Woodford helped immeasurably by his attitude towards writing. It was a craft, he said, to be learned and the writer must be willing to spend as much time on it as a doctor does learning his craft, or the dentist or lawyer. It was always tough at first, he said, but then what wasn't. "Be thankful it's tough," he said in effect, "or the woods would be full of writers and nobody could make a decent living."

I guess it was Woodford, really, who kept me at it. The monotonous return of manuscripts and rejection slips had almost finished me. I was disillusioned and just plain tired. It was getting very difficult to run a clean sheet of paper into the typewriter and begin all over again. Reading Woodford revived all my enthusiasm. I'll always be grateful to him for that.

But I didn't follow his advice. He said the best bet for the beginning writer was the novel. After all, 70,000 words is just ten short stories and you don't have to dream up ten sets of characters, plots, locales, incidents, complications and so on. One set will do. You just drag the whole thing out more and give more detail.

I decided on a sort of half-way measure. I'd quit writing the short-short stories all right, but I wouldn't go for the full-length novel either. Instead I'd try a sort of double length story for the confession magazines. There were plenty of them on the market and they were most popular, as though reading about somebody else's troubles somehow made your own easier.

The formula was pretty simple – sin, suffering, repentance and redemption. The story was always told in the first person – usually by a girl who had sinned, but it could be a man and she/he was always terribly sorry for what he'd done. A hot seduction scene was a must so that the reader could have a good time while learning that sin and sex didn't pay.

I decided to make it pay. You had to sign an affidavit to the effect that the story was true, but then "true" is a word with many interpretations. True to life would do. Or true in the sense that it illustrated a "moral" truth. There was nothing to say it had to be literally factual.

Just at that time the Saskatoon *Star-Phoenix* ran a news item more bizarre than any true story ever written. It concerned a twenty-eight-year-old hired farm hand who had written and sold a story to one of the confession magazines and had received the unbelievable sum of $475 for it. Then he had gone to the city, got a room in a hotel on First Avenue, liquor and a whore, and made a night of it. But after the long, lonely winter on the farm it was too much for him. Suffering from what the doctors called "delusions of persecution and disease phobia," he'd run amok, jumped through a large window and run bleeding and screaming down the street. The judge sent him to the Battleford Mental Hospital.

I had some idea of how the poor guy felt. All those long, lone nights in a dingy room, probably working by the light of a coal-oil lamp, he sat and wrote and re-wrote and re-wrote. All very secret. Then he sent it off and had it accepted and was required to sign the affidavit of its truthfulness. The dream of the city – wine, women and song –

new clothing. But brooding over the affidavit and the fear of venereal disease finally drove him over the edge. The irony of it.

I wrote a short story based on the incident and sent it off to *Esquire*. I read it again just the other day. I still can't see why they refused it. Probably thought it was too far-fetched.

So I decided to write a true confession story of my own and I, too, got into trouble.

Sin, Sex and Suffering. That should be easy to write about for Wannego was full of it. But finding a story was another thing. I needed a plot. Well, why not a school teacher? Some teachers were overcome with lust for nubile young maidens, and there were some nice, juicy stories about that.

There was, for example, the principal who had been at Wannego two principals before Harry King. He was a bachelor of about thirty-five, a sombre, smoldering man. He kept a thirteen-year-old child in after school one evening and raped her on the cloakroom floor. The poor girl went screaming home – they lived just across the road from the school – and told her parents what had happened. Her father, a most respectable man of good standing in the community, was so shamed that he took no action against the principal but locked his daughter in her room and wouldn't let her out. One night about a week later the big frame house caught on fire. There was, of course, no fire department in Wannego, but all the neighbours came with buckets to help extinguish the fire. They could see the girl standing at her window and screaming, but no one could get to her. The parents left town and were never heard of again. The principal left at the end of the term.

No, I decided, I couldn't use that story. No repentance, or redemption either.

Then there was the story of Paul Nufordt who ran a lumberyard in town. Paul was in very solid with the government then in power and was given as a reward for his services the job of weed inspector. Trying to eradicate weeds in Saskatchewan during the Thirties was like trying to combat mosquitoes in a swamp with a fly swatter. Weeds were about the only thing that would grow. Russian thistle was everywhere. Thriving on the drought, it got the jump on the wheat in the spring and after that the wheat never had a chance. In the fall the big bushy plants broke off and blew across the fields, spreading millions of seeds as they went.

So the weed inspector usually made out a few reports, drew his meagre salary and didn't bother anybody. Not Paul. His great enemy in the district was Joe Rodin, who had a miserable farm north of town, and who had decided that since wheat was worthless anyway he might as well just let the weeds grow and live on relief. Paul charged Joe with violating the noxious weed act, with the result that he was hauled into court and fined ten dollars.

So what had been a smouldering feud became active. Rodin and his friends took to hanging around Paul's lumberyard, hurling insults and stones, while Paul took to sitting in his office with a loaded shotgun close at hand. One night, juiced to the eyebrows, Joe and his boys became careless, advanced to the lumberyard office and threw a brick through the big front window. Then they ran like hell. Paul raised his shotgun and let Joe have both barrels right in the backside.

The noise of the shooting brought Constable Broadfoot to the scene and he prevented the Rodin boys from going after Paul and persuaded them to take care of their father who was lying in the street with a backside full of shotgun pellets. Finally they got a grain door from the elevator and loaded him into the back of a truck and took him to the hospital at Wakaw. But he died.

Broadfoot showed me a picture they'd taken of Rodin's posterior for evidence and it was indeed a mess. The police had to charge Nufordt with something for the shooting. The court's verdict was "justifiable homicide" and the penalty was one year suspended sentence. What really dumb-founded Broadfoot about the case was that Rodin's relatives later put in a bill to the government to cover the expense of hauling Joe to the hospital.

No, that one wouldn't do either. Suffering and sin, yes, but no sex. Not a lot of repentance and redemption either.

I thought of using Ruby's story, but soon realized it wouldn't do. The confession books used stories about girls who'd "made one fatal mistake," not happy whores like Ruby. Besides, incest was a taboo with the confession books that always maintained a high moral tone.

And then one afternoon when I'd dismissed my English class I noticed that Heather Lopynski was still in her seat.

"What is it, Heather?" I asked. "I don't remember asking you to remain after school."

"You didn't," she said. "But I want to talk to you. Please, can I talk to you?"

I had noticed Heather Lopynski the very first day of school. She was small and lithe and beautiful with dark hair and huge, inquisitive eyes. Although she was only fifteen, she was already in Grade Eleven and was far and away the brightest student in the room.

She was the kind of student that every teacher appreci-ates, industrious, inquisitive, lively, co-operative. Whatever was going on, from a class party to a botany outing, she greeted with enthusiasm. She didn't make a big fuss about it or become a nuisance, she just enjoyed doing it. If a teacher had a roomful of pupils like Heather, teaching would be great. If in ten years of teaching you get two like her you are lucky.

None of the other teachers seemed terribly impressed with the family – there were no less than six of them going to school – and when I'd mention Heather they'd say, "Oh yes . . . the Lopynski gang," and shake their heads sadly.

One afternoon Heather's mother had come to see me. She

rapped shyly on the door after the kids were gone and asked if she might talk to me. I invited her to sit down and closed the classroom door to shut out the sound from the hall.

She sat in the front seat and crossed her legs. She had the most attractive legs, I noticed, and they were attached to a most attractive body. But it wasn't her good looks that impressed me most about Mrs. Lopynski – it was her presence. Sex appeal came from that woman like a charge of electricity. There was no part of her that was particularly sexy; it was just everything. Eyes, hair, mouth, complexion, build, gestures, all combined to give a man one idea and one idea only.

"Uh . . . what is it you want to see me about, Mrs. Lopynski?"

"Oh, please call me Blanche, everybody else does. I want to ask you about Heather."

"Yes, well Heather is getting along very well. She's . . ."

I stopped because somebody had opened the classroom door at the back of the room. But nobody entered. Just pushed the door well open and left it at that.

"I know she's getting along well," Mrs. Lopynski frowned prettily. "But I think she's working too hard."

"Oh?"

"Yes, she does so much homework and then, of course, helps me with the housework. And she's not strong, you know."

"No, I didn't know."

"Oh yes . . . as a little girl she was very sick with pleurisy . . . for a long time . . . and . . . well, we watch her carefully. I wouldn't want her to get it again."

"Of course not. She doesn't need to work so hard. She's away ahead of her class now."

Harry King poked his head into the room then, looked hard at Blanche Lopynski and said, "Oh excuse me, I didn't know you were busy."

Mrs. Lopynski got up. "I must be going anyway. Thank

you for talking to me." She swished out past Harry, who closed the door behind her and advanced to my desk.

"What in hell is the idea?" he demanded.

"What idea?"

"Closing the door when you've got that woman in your room!"

"Oh . . . was it you opened the door?"

"I sure as hell did. Boy!"

"Look, I may be pretty obtuse, but I don't know what you are talking about. She's the parent of one of our students."

"She's the parent of half the students in this school. The only trouble is she hasn't got a husband."

"But . . . she's Mrs. . . . Mrs. Lopynski."

"Did you ever see Mr. Lopynski?"

"No . . . but then there are lots of people I haven't met."

"There is no Mr. Lopynski. If there ever was one he left years ago and has never been back."

"I don't get it."

"Well, she does, and plenty. Every one of those kids in the school and the three at home have got a different Daddy. . . ."

"Jesus Christ."

"Oh maybe some of them have the same father, but there's no way of telling. Our Blanche is a very loving woman."

"But the kids are all dressed well, clean, and such nice kids, too."

"Oh she's a good mother all right. Takes damned good care of her kids. And she's a nice enough person, too. But she just can't keep her legs together. The woman has no morals at all. People keep saying that something should be done about it. But what? Take the kids away and put them in some kind of institution? They seem happy where they are. They're among the best behaved and smartest kids in school. They've just learned the facts of life earlier than most is all."

"Maybe Heather doesn't know what's going on. It's possible."

"Sure . . . if she were deaf and blind and a moron . . . which she isn't. I don't know . . ." he scratched his chin, "I often wonder about those kids. . . ."

"Nine kids. How can a woman have nine kids and look so young and so . . ."

"Sexy? She's that, all right. She can't be more than thirty-five or so. There's two sets of twins in that bunch. Well, they say having kids is good for a woman's looks. She proves it."

So when Heather Lopynski said she wanted to talk to me I thought back to that conversation, as I had many times in the past year and a half. What part did she play in her mother's life, I wondered. Outwardly she was a sweet, well-adjusted child. But how could she be? As I looked down at her now she was frowning into a book on her desk. I closed my record book with a snap, walked down the aisle and sat on the desk in front of her.

She looked up at me. "Mr. Braithwaite, my mother wants me to go to the city to school."

"Oh? Do you want to?"

"No, not at all. One of her friends wants me to come and live at his house and help look after his two small children. He's quite rich. He says his wife wants me to come, too."

"And you don't want to."

Her eyes were very direct. "No. I don't like this man at all. He's been after me two times already."

"In what way?"

"He wants to have me. Mother never lets any of us children be around when her friends come to call, but he came once when she was out working for Mr. McNab. He asked me to sit on his knee and then he began to feel all over me." She was looking down at the desk now and a blush was spreading over her pale face.

"When was this?"

"About a month ago. He tried to hold me but I got away from him and went outside."

"Did you tell anyone about it? Your mother?"

"No. I was too ashamed. Besides, this man is very generous to my mother. I don't know what we'd do if he stopped coming around. And now he wants me to go and live at his house."

"Have any of your mother's other friends bothered you?"

"Yes," it was a whisper. "There was one once . . . when I was twelve . . . at a party . . . he was very drunk. He got me out of bed where I was with my sister and tried to make me do it with him. But I ran away and hid in a coal shed all night down by the track. I just had my nightie on and it was terribly cold. I was sick for a long time afterwards." Her face had gone white but she was not crying.

Good Lord! I thought, this child, this little sweet-natured child. "You can't stay in that house any more," I said.

"But I must stay. I don't want to go to the city with my mother's friend." Then she got up. "I must go now. My mother needs me." Before I could protest she had gathered her books together and slipped out the door.

I talked to Harry King about it.

"Don't get involved," he said. "You're hired here as a teacher, not a social worker."

"Somebody's got to do something."

"Why? These people have been getting along like that for years. And they'll keep on doing it."

"I'm going to the police," I said.

"Do you want them to arrest this man? What's the charge?"

"Well . . . uh . . . carnal knowledge of a juvenile."

"He didn't do it. The girl says he patted her. She can't even prove *that*. Have you any idea what a smart defence lawyer could do to that kid on the witness stand? With her mother's reputation?"

"How about that other . . . the man who tried to rape her?"

"Four years ago. Better forget about that one . . . if it ever happened."

"What do you mean?"

"Heather has quite an imagination, you know. Reads a lot. She may be making the whole thing up."

"No . . . no . . . she's not making it up. I know that."

"You don't know. Besides, these people don't know any other way to live."

"Oh sure . . . and I suppose they really like it. That's a nice way to get out of doing anything about it."

Harry's jaw muscles began to twitch. "Just keep out of it, Max. Don't get involved. It could lead to a lot of trouble."

"How?"

"Well, there are more people mixed up with that family than you think. Just leave them alone. They don't cause any trouble."

"But Heather doesn't want to go to the city to live."

"Of course she doesn't. What kid of fifteen does want to leave her family. But it might be the best thing in the world for her. Chance to get away from this lousy set-up. There's another angle . . . girls that age often fall for their teachers."

"Oh come on."

"Especially if their teachers are young and sympathetic. It's a possibility, you know. Better be careful." He put on his black fedora and left.

Well, here I was right in the middle of the damnedest melodrama that no soap opera writer could improve on. And then a strange and rather bad thing began to happen to me. I became more interested in Heather Lopynski's dilemma as a story than as a real-life problem.

And this is what happens with every writer. At some point in every situation he begins to think of it as a story. It doesn't matter how intimate it is or whom it involves – friends, parents, wife, children – what happens to them sooner or later becomes *material*. Somerset Maugham, the greatest story teller of my generation, once said that sooner or later everything that had ever happened to him was used in his writing.

It's a terrible thing in a way. To be always sort of sitting apart watching what is happening to you and to those about you and storing it away for future use. But it is natural, too. For a writer can only write that which he knows. He must start with that. Invention is important but there must be a board from which invention can spring. To labour the comparison, fancy twists and turns in the air are not possible without that springboard to set them going.

It's a game, really. All fiction writers are caught in adolescence, playing games of make-believe. "What if" is really the key phrase. What if this had happened instead of that? What if when Jones went to pick up his bride he'd had a flat tire and met Mary? What if, what if, what if – the possibilities are endless and the writer, the manipulator, provides them.

The story I wrote about Heather Lopynski and her mother was a dilly. Twenty thousand words of sex, sin, suffering. What if she fell in love with me, Harry King asked. What if, indeed. And what if I tried to help her and in helping her had compromised myself with her and there was I, a married man with the sweetest, most understanding, most loveable wife in the world and I was deceiving her. I knew it was wrong. All my father's teaching and my Sunday School teachers and good pastor Alexander – all told me I was wrong. I prayed for help, but something stronger than my own will had me in thrall. They want hokum, I said. Hokum is what they'll get.

I have the story here before me now. It's called "Putty in My Hands!" How does that grab you for a title? It is signed with the name Daryl Morganson and it begins with the sentence: "I'm sure if I had known the influence of a loving mother I never could have treated Lorrie as I did." Then there are eighty more pages of the same, ending with complete redemption.

Aileen typed it out for me. There are great advantages to a writer in having his wife type his stuff. In the first place, not only could I not type but I couldn't spell. Punctuation and grammar I knew. I'd learned to type during the long winter evenings the first year I was teaching in the rural school and boarding on a farm. There was nothing else to do. Couldn't read because of the lousy light, no radio, no television. So I rented a typewriter with blank keys, bought a book of instructions and set about to learn the touch system. But I never quite finished the course with the result that my typing has a decidedly unfinished quality about it.

Another advantage is that Aileen is the best judge of writing I know. I hover about when she's typing and if I hear her chuckle now and then I know I've hit just the right touch. If, on the other hand, she leans back in her chair and sighs, gets irritable, makes mistakes, I know that I'm in for some re-writing.

When Aileen was typing "Putty in My Hands" she neither chuckled nor sighed. She was aghast. I kept hearing mumbled expletives like "Oh really!" or "Not again!" or "How phony can you get?"

"This will never sell," she said when it was typed.

"Why not? It's got all the ingredients . . . sin, suffering, sex . . ."

"It hasn't got the most essential ingredient . . . sincerity."

"Come on. That story is so sincere that it's sickening."

"That's right. You don't believe what you are saying."

She was right, of course. I sent it away to the confession magazine and they sent it right back. They said it lacked sincerity.

And right there I learned another thing. There is no such thing as successful tongue-in-cheek writing. People used to say to me (and they still do), "Oh those little love stories are simple. Just learn the boy-meets-girl formula, put your tongue in your cheek and go to it. Make a million if you want to prostitute your art."

I don't believe it. I believe that life-is-real-life-is-earnest stories are written by people who believe just that. No matter how sophisticated and worldly they may seem, they are sentimental slobs at heart. God *is* in his heaven and all *is* right with the world so far as they are concerned. True love always does win out. The good *do* prosper and the bad *are* punished. There is a Santa Claus, all men are created equal, justice does triumph. Deep down in their hearts they believe these things. Otherwise they couldn't say so with conviction.

And that is the reason the cute little happy-ending stories have all but disappeared from our magazines. We are finally shaking loose from the Cinderella, Santa Claus myths. We are at last beginning to look at things the way they are. What we see often isn't very nice . . . corruption, pollution, bigotry, and worst of all hypocrisy. People prate about a "just society" and we say "Where?" Looking at the mess and really seeing it is the first step towards doing something about it.

Maybe it's just as well that story didn't sell. The mind boggles at what might have happened if it had. Why I might have gone to New York and become a successful magazine fiction writer and I might have got all involved with that fast society down there and I might have – it's too ghastly to think on.

What about Heather Lopynski? Well, we did help her. By chance we heard of a nice respectable family in Saskatoon who needed a girl to work for her board and where the husband was too tired to chase anybody. She worked hard and went on to university and became a high school teacher. She got married finally and one day Aileen met her in a store in Saskatoon. She said she was happy.

But gosh she was a beautiful girl. What if . . .

I had learned to play auction bridge when I was in high school, but during the years I taught in rural schools there was little opportunity to play any kind of bridge. In Wannego I was introduced to the wonders and intricacies of contract bridge. It was not an altogether happy introduction.

Card-playing has always been important in Saskatchewan. As a kid I spent many long winter evenings by the flickering light of the coal-oil lamp playing rummy, old maid, or snap with my brothers and sisters. These were replaced, as we grew older with whist, euchre, five-hundred and, finally, auction bridge.

In Aileen's family they play a game which I'm sure Bob Treleaven must have invented, called "Blackout." It would be impossible for me to outline all the intricacies of this contest here, but a great deal of laughing and cursing are an integral part of it. Any number can play, each player being dealt one card on the first deal, two on the second, three on the third and on up while the cards last. You declare how many tricks you think you can take with a given hand and if you take more or less than that number you "blackout." It's a "gang-up" game, with everybody trying to make the highest player blackout and it can become pretty vicious. Those who make their bids squeal with glee while those who don't shout "Oh hell!"

The most ardent card player I ever knew, though, was Homer Willoughby who ran one of the elevators in Wannego. Since there was little wheat being hauled he had plenty of time on his hands. He spent it hanging around the restaurant or the hotel lobby and in the inside pocket of his jacket he always had a long wooden cribbage board.

If you happened to stop near him he'd produce the board and a pack of cards, nudge you gently, lift his cheek in an exaggerated wink and say, "How about a little game?"

If you protested that you didn't have time, that you had to catch a bus or a store before it closed he'd say, "This won't take long," and begin dealing the cards. He was right, too. It never did take long. Before you knew it he'd fifteen-two'd you out of the game and your dime and was cutting the cards for another deal.

He would do this anywhere – in the post office, the general store, the bank, even on the street. If you paused for a second he had you. His greatest triumph, it was said, though I find it hard to believe, was when he engaged the preacher in a game on the way out of church one Sunday. The parson held out his hand to shake Homer's and got instead a cribbage hand. Some claim Homer won half the collection before the preacher could shake him.

In Wannego, besides the constant smear games in the hotel and the poker games in the livery barn, whist drives were organized by church groups to buy new choir gowns and euchre tournaments were common. But we sophisticates eschewed all of these mundane games and took up contract bridge.

As everyone knows by now, the game was developed from auction bridge in 1925 by Harold S. Vanderbilt when he and some friends were playing auction bridge on board ship. He subsequently introduced it to the New York clubs, where it was played almost exclusively until Ely Culbertson got hold of it and, by some of the slickest promotion in history, developed it into the world's leading card game.

Culbertson was everywhere in the Thirties. His long, lean face peered at you from newspapers and magazines. The *Reader's Digest* frequently ran articles about him. His syndicated columns reached millions and he even taught bridge playing by radio. I remember a movie short in which he demonstrated how, by stacking the deck, a grand slam could be made with a hand that held few of the high cards. It was very impressive, but I'm blessed if I can remember how it is done.

Contract Bridge came to Wannego in the mid-Thirties and soon became an obsession. Everybody wanted to get into the act. People with no more card sense than a rabbit drove other people crazy trying to play the game. This was particularly true of the bridge club we organized. We had all kinds, from Yvonne Beltier who had played duplicate bridge in the city to Edna Petrie who, I swear, during the four months the club lasted, had no notion whatsoever what card game we were playing, if indeed she knew that we were playing cards at all.

Besides the Petries, ourselves and the Beltiers there was Ernest Stoneman and his wife, Beulah. (The Kings much preferred playing smear. Harry was convinced, I'm sure, that there was something unmanly about bridge, perhaps un-British, too.) So, as they say in drama club circles, we had a well-orchestrated cast. There were bold players, timid players, sneaky players and those who said, constantly, "What the hell? It's only a game."

Larry Petrie was a sneaky player. As often as not he'd open the bidding with, "Let me see now . . . I think . . . I'll bid clubs – for now."

This had the advantage of being non-committal. He hadn't said how many clubs, and he'd indicated to his partner that he might be pretty strong in other suits. Sneaky.

Let's say his opponent bid one spade.

This would bring the bidding around to Edna Petrie who had been sitting there talking about the colour of her new kitchen curtains. When informed that it was her turn to bid, she would frown deeply at the interruption and look at her hand as though she had never seen it before, which indeed she hadn't, and begin to arrange the cards in some sort of order. Then she would say, "What did you people bid?"

On being advised that the opening bid was one club, she would begin to count the clubs in her hand by pointing to them one after the other with a long, bony finger and muttering under her breath, "I don't see how they can bid *spades*. What did you bid partner?"

"One club."

"One club! Well . . ." Now she would count the spades, also by pointing to them one at a time. "I don't really think . . . oh . . . clubs. That's supposed to mean something, isn't it?"

"Sometimes."

"But I can never remember what it means. Well, I guess I'll bid spades."

"That's what they bid."

"Oh . . . then I can't bid it again, can I. Well, I pass."

When she'd finally lay down her hand it would be full of diamonds.

"Why didn't you bid diamonds?" her husband would ask.

"Because they're not as high as spades, silly."

"You could have bid two."

"But I couldn't bid against you."

And there the argument would end. Something strange happened when Larry and Edna happened to be partners. An attitude developed that was completely foreign to this perfectly happy couple. Something that I didn't like.

For Larry Petrie had one bad vice. Normally a quiet, non-aggressive man, the bridge club revealed a hitherto suppressed passion for gambling.

I have seen this gambling obsession turn up in other odd places. When I was head schoolmaster at H.M.C.S. *York* in Toronto I had on my staff a quiet, unassuming, studious man who everybody thought had no vices at all. But he had one. All day he'd sit at his desk while the ratings worked away at arithmetic problems, or slept, or matched quarters in the back seats, and he'd make marks on a piece of paper. Everyone took it for granted that he was preparing lessons or marking papers, but actually he was doping the races for the weekend meet at Woodbine or Lansdowne park.

He was hooked on racehorse gambling as anyone has ever been hooked on dope. Whenever the horses were running he was there, trying out the system he'd so carefully worked out when he was supposed to be teaching. In the wardroom he'd explain this system to anyone who'd listen. It was always absolutely fool-proof. Couldn't miss. All that was necessary, he'd explain, was to stick to the system.

Invariably after the day he'd be asked by someone how the system had stood up.

"Great. Exactly as I worked it out."

"Then you made a lot of money?"

"No."

"How come?"

"Well, there was this long shot in the third that really should have won . . . but . . . it didn't. But the system was great."

It was always the same story. Instead of making the four hundred dollars he'd have made by following his system, he lost sixty-five. But it never cured him.

Larry Petrie was of the same genre. A gambling fiend lurking behind the benign facade of a contented school-teacher. As soon as the members of the bridge club would assemble (we played alternately at each other's houses) and the tables were set up and the salted peanuts and sticky candy were in place, Larry would sit up, rub his hands together, breathe a little faster and say, "We should really play for a little money. You know . . . tenth of a cent a point or something like that . . . ha, ha."

Before any of us could comment on that, Edna, who knew his weakness, would disclaim, "I should say not. If you want to gamble go down to the livery barn and play poker."

"I was only kidding. You know that."

"Ha! When it comes to gambling you have no self-mastery."

Edna was great on self-mastery. She'd been raised by an aunt who was very strict and Edna remained true to her principles. She was strong against swearing, drinking, gambling, sex and all the other sins. On the rare occasion when somebody could afford a bottle we had to be careful that Edna didn't surreptitiously pick up half-empty glasses and pour the booze down the sink. A terrible thing to do at any time but in those hard days a dastardly crime.

The Beltiers were an interesting bridge couple. Yvonne played with the skill and precision of a true duplicate bridger while Danny showed a decidedly cavalier attitude towards the game. Because of his short-sightedness he never knew exactly what was in his hand and he had the titillating habit of bidding three no trump after everybody else had passed.

"Well, I guess it's time for three no trump," he'd announce happily just as everyone else was throwing in their hand. Yvonne never criticized him out loud for this. A fine-line frown would cross her forehead as she laid down her hand and looked for a magazine to read. The most annoying part of this performance was that, often as not, he'd make the damned bid.

But it was as a kibitzer that Danny really excelled. When he was dummy, which was often, he'd wander between the tables to check on the other players. A good kibitzer should be able to see the cards at least from a slightly bent position. Danny had to lean over the player's shoulder and get his eyes so close to the cards that all the player could see was the curly black hair on the back of Danny's head. By the time he'd got around the table and inspected all the hands – otherwise how could he gauge the play? – the game tended to be somewhat disrupted.

Beulah and Ernest Stoneman played the game strictly according to their natures. Beulah was quiet and contemplative; Ernest loud and disgusted. He hated the game and played it only because he hated reading or listening to the radio even more. He cursed his hand loudly if it were bad, banged on the table and filled his mouth with salted peanuts. If his hand were good, he'd tilt his chair away back – many a wooden chair collapsed under the strain – grin broadly and say, "Now, by gawd, this is more like it. What do you say there, partner? Let's go get 'em."

As often as not his partner would pass, and then he'd come forward with a roar, banging the chair legs down and bashing the table with his elbows. "How in the name of hell can you pass when I've got a hand like this?"

Aileen played the game shrewdly and well; I played it shrewdly and terrible. I caught on to the fundamentals of the game quickly enough and sometimes I could even apply them. My trouble consisted of mental blind spots and complete lack of interest which anyone who has ever lived with a writer will recognize. It's caused by constructing plots and devising dialogue when you should be concentrating on the matter in hand.

The bridge club lasted most of one winter and then, one cold, miserable night in March, it came to a terrible end.

March is the worst month of the year in Saskatchewan. It always seems that the long, cold winter should be ending by March and it never does. November isn't bad because winter begins then and there is always the fascination of the changing seasons. The first snow comes and it's clean and new and fresh. Kids chase each other through it and make fox and goose trails. Dogs frolic in it, and there is even some fun in the crunch it makes beneath your overshoes on wooden sidewalks.

December is saved by Christmas. January is bad, cold and windy and long. The relentless winds whine around the windows and blow in through the cracks. Pumps freeze up and snow piles high over the path to the backhouse. The brown stain of slops grows bigger and bigger at the back door and the coal in the bin shrinks at a great rate.

February is worse. That's when old horses in the fields

give up and lie down in the lee of strawstacks and die. You can hear the coyotes tearing at their frozen carcasses at night. Old humans, too, often quit during February. The winter is just too long for them. Their tired old bones can't take it any more and, after the long, struggling years, they lie down peacefully and pass on to whatever reward awaits them.

And then comes the first thaw of March. The snow goes soft. Brown horse-turds show up in the deep rutted road; snow melts away from the side of the house, thus giving up its insulating quality; water drips from the eaves to form long spears of ice that reach the ground. And people say, "It's come at last. Spring is here. We've survived another winter."

But March is only playing one of her dirty little tricks. The cold winds come again and blow clear through the house where the banking has melted away and exposed it. The wind rises to gale force and shrieks and howls about the corners, tearing at the shingles, raising the crusted snow and dust into the air. Often new snow comes and joins the old so that the air is so full of swirling snow and dust that a man dare not venture the length of his own yard. Winter is taking its last savage bite. The March blizzards are the cruelest of the whole winter.

It was during one of these wretched evenings that we had the bridge club at our house. "I wonder if anyone will come out on a night like this," Aileen pondered as she waxed the linoleum floor.

"Oh they'll come," I said. "What else is there to do? I hope they all bring sweaters. I can't keep this house warm."

I was right. They came, each bringing with him his own hate against the weather and the hard times. Each with nerve ends rubbed raw with the promise of spring so cruelly snatched away.

And it was then that, when Larry Petrie suggested that we liven things up a bit by playing for small stakes, nobody, not even his wife, objected. We were all feeling mean enough to want to humiliate and deprive even our best friends. So we settled on a tenth of a cent a point and began the game.

People who can't afford to lose a little money shouldn't gamble, and not one of us could afford to lose a plugged nickel. Now the whole game took on an entirely different aspect. The peccadilloes and idiosyncrasies of the players that had been highly amusing at best and slightly annoying at worst now became terrible.

Right off we established the rule that there would be no talking across the table, and that was like tying the hands of a deaf mute. None of us but Yvonne knew anything of the neat little systems by which bridge players tell each other the nature of their hands. We could only sit, glum and suspicious, furtively peering at each other from the corner of our eyes, vainly trying to glean a straw of information.

It was a weird evening, as I remember it. The fierce west wind raging outside and the storms of avarice raging within. Gone was the easy banter and gay laughter that came when some fool play was made, replaced by grim, tight-lipped mutterings and fearful scowls. As luck in bridge often does, it all ran one way. Ernest Stoneman, the only man with a decent salary, got all the good luck, while Larry Petrie whose salary was less than mine got all the bad. And the worse his luck got the more desperate and intense he became.

We've simply got to stop this," Aileen whispered to me in the kitchen. We had finished our rubber with the Beltiers and broken about even.

"How?" I asked.

"I could serve lunch."

"Try it."

So Aileen announced in a gay but firm tone that lunch would be served.

"Can't until we finish the rubber," Petrie snarled. He had just been set on a four spade bid, doubled, and dropped five hundred points. Which, added to the two dollars he'd already lost, would make a real hole in his budget.

So, there was nothing to do but watch the two couples fight it out. While the coffee perked away on the kitchen stove we watched them deal and bid and pass and their faces grow grey with the strain. Then it happened.

Out of the deck of cards came four of those crazy hands that can sometimes turn up in this crazy game. I can see them yet. The men had all the good cards, the women nothing. Larry had no less than ten spades from the king down to the deuce with only the ten and five missing. Edna had the ace and the five. Yvonne had no spades at all and Ernest, who was on Larry's right, had the lone ten.

Ernest had the other three aces and a long string of hearts including the top honour cards. It was clearly a fight between Larry and Ernest. And that's exactly what it was – a fight. For now all their natural antipathy for each other came boiling to the surface. Each disliked the other's type immensely. Ernest called men like Larry egghead milksops, while to Larry Ernest was an insensitive bully. And there, in our tiny house, with the March winds fussing outside, the battle was joined.

The rest of us stood around uncertain and unhappy. There was no way to stop it. Larry saw his chance to win back the money he'd lost. It was more like a poker game than a bridge game. Up and up went the bidding – four, five, six – and then Ernest banged the table with a big fist and declared, "Grand slam in hearts. God damn it beat that!"

Larry was shaking like the fender of a Model-T. He wiped his face, carefully laid his cards on the table and said, "Grand slam in spades. God damn it beat *that*."

It was the first time any of us had heard him swear, but not the last.

Ernest couldn't take that – not from a milksop. I think

for a moment he thought he was playing poker and could bluff his way out. Anyway, to the surprise of the kibitzers and the horror of his wife, he banged the table even harder and bellowed, "Grand slam in no trump."

"Double!"

"Redouble!"

Then, as the realization of what he'd done came upon him, his face became very red, his jaw muscles jumped and for a split second it looked as though he would hit somebody. Instead he glanced at his wife and that quieted him. Something there told him all would be well.

Slowly and deliberately Larry led the nine of spades and held his breath. Where was that ace? Yvonne laid down her hand. It wasn't there. Ernest blanched. He was done for. From the dummy he played a small club.

Now it was Edna's play and she was terrified. She was seeing a new Larry and what she saw dismayed her. All through the bidding it was this and not the disposition of cards that had absorbed her mind. Now she began to think, and that was a mistake.

From the fragments of bridge lore that had filtered into her mind in the past months she tried to pick one that would fit the occasion. There was something about third player playing high – or was it low. Oh dear. And aces, they always confused her. In one of the rare occasions when she'd paid some attention to the game she'd seen Yvonne hold back an ace and everyone had commented on what an astute play it had been. Oh dear. She wished people would say something and not stare so. "She who hesitates is lost," she mumbled sickly, and played the five.

Ernest took the trick with the ten and all the other tricks after it. That is, he would have taken all the tricks, but he never got the chance. Larry Petrie flew screaming into the air when the ten was played and upset the bridge table, spilling candy and cards all over the floor. In a few brief but concise sentences he went over his married life with Edna and it was plain that inherent in their relationship had been a certain amount of frustration. He referred to her family and the wedding and even to the matter of their having no children. Then, without pausing he threw a five-dollar bill onto the coffee table, grabbed his coat and tore out into the storm.

We persuaded Edna, who by now was bawling like a baby, that she should stay with us for the night and sleep on our couch. In silence we ate our salmon sandwiches and drank our coffee. Then the Stoneman's left, saying that under no circumstances would they take Larry's money. It had all been in fun.

The next day Edna was subdued and pensive. At breakfast she ignored her food and sat thinking. She had learned something about her husband that she'd never suspected. He actually could get mad. Maybe he'd hated her all along and only his mild nature had kept him from blowing up long before this. For the first time in her life she was unsure of this seemingly mild, inoffensive, non-aggressive man.

Larry dropped in on his way to school. He was bewildered and mumblingly apologetic. I guess he'd learned something about himself, too, that he'd never suspected. Behind the apologies and bustle of getting ready to go, we noticed them looking at each other speculatively. Never again would they be completely sure of each other. I suspect their marriage improved immensely.

Spring came shortly after that. Crows cawed from the poplar trees and horned larks carolled on the wing. The sun shone, the snow melted, the frogs sang in the sloughs. Winter had finally let go. The time for long evenings had come with gardening and tennis and walks on the rutted roads. There was no more time for bridge and our little club never met again.

Most people when they think of the Royal Canadian
Mounted Police think of a tall, beautiful figure in a trim
uniform, or the musical ride, or "they always get their
man," or, if they're old enough, of Nelson Eddy singing
to Jeannette McDonald. I always think of dusty Ford V-8
cars, bootleg whiskey, and the night we stole Sir Percival
Ardley's convertible.

During the Thirties the RCMP were the only police in
rural Saskatchewan. They were the town constable, the
local sheriff, the captain of detectives, the traffic cop, the
highway patrol, the FBI, the chief of police all rolled into
one. They were kept busy during the depression helping
to quell riots, chasing bums – anybody who didn't have a
job – off railway property, keeping tabs on the communists
who were trying to undermine our free society. Depending
on where you stood, the Mounties were respected, revered,
feared or detested. As far as we were concerned, they were
an important part of our social set.

Along with Sergeant Stoneman there were three constables in Wannego. They came and went even more frequently than school teachers and now and then there would
be a romance with one of the local girls. The three I
remember best I will call Nikochuk, McAdam, and Ardley.
They were all single, all boarded at the hotel, and were all
three excellent chaps. Well – practically all three.

Nichochuk was a friendly Ukrainian, who got along
well with everybody. McAdam was a tall blond Scotsman
with a great deal of boyish charm who like to knit. He
came to Wannego fresh from a three-year stint in the Arctic
and he said that knitting was his way of putting in the
time. If this were true, then half the Eskimo women in his

territory must have been wearing woollen sweaters, for that was the only thing he ever knitted. They required a lot of fitting, those sweaters, and my best memory of McAdam is of him pulling a sweater on or off a well-rounded female torso and patting it here and there to check the fit.

McAdam could speak the Eskimo tongue, too. At least he could say a number of words that involved a great deal of lip-pursing, which he generously taught to the young ladies.

McAdam was a good source of material. He told me some lively incidents and I gleefully wrote them into short stories and sent them to editors, thinking that if there was anything they knew about Canada it was Mounties. But none of the stories sold and I realized later that I wasn't presenting the traditional Mountie – sharp profile, round hat, high boots, Sam Browne belt, sleek bay horse and all – galloping across the plains, relentlessly following renegade Indians, never ceasing until he got his man. Mounties doing regular police work were to them "unrealistic."

One day when Aileen and Beryl were in Saskatoon and I was taking my meals in the hotel dining room, I was eating with Sandy McAdam when he said,

"Say, can you smell something?"

"Just this cheese omelette."

"No, I mean something else." He took a long sniff. "Yeah, it's still there."

I took a deep sniff. "You mean that sort of sour, putrid smell?"

"Correct. It's coming from my tunic. I've used everything I know on it, and I thought I'd got it all out. Evidently I didn't."

Then he told me this story.

For years the police at the Wannego detachment had been trying to get the goods on an old bootlegger named Anton Vrom. Vrom was a bachelor and lived in a dilapitated shack on a little knoll west of town. There were no real hills in the Wannego area, so that from the top of this knoll you could see about five miles of the dirt road leading to his place. Any car coming along that road could easily be spotted by Anton and by the time the police got there no evidence was to be found.

Each newcomer to the detachment was given the job of trying to catch old Anton. One tried driving up at night with no lights but ran into the ditch and had to walk back to town. Another borrowed a horse and tried coming across the fields, but prairie chickens and magpies that flew up at his approach warned the old rascal and all the Mountie got out of it was a sore backside.

Sandy McAdam had tried several times to catch Anton but had never made it. Invariably when he got to the shack the old man was sitting in his rickety chair beside his dirty table smoking a ragged cigaret and waiting for him. He'd grin his rotten-toothed grin and say, "Hello, Mr. Policeman. Nice of you to call."

But the Scots are a determined breed and Sandy refused to give up. There were more fights on the front street and more rotten home-brew in circulation which had the unmistakable stench of that produced by old Anton. Finally Sandy decided that he would walk out to Anton's place and catch him that way. He'd carry no light. In the Arctic he'd got pretty accustomed to travelling in the dark.

So he set out along the road, walking mostly in the ditch. Away off he could see the light of Anton's coal-oil lamp burning in the single room of the shack. It took him almost two hours to reach the yard. Then he had to be careful, for the wily old rascal had rigged up a system of wires attached to old rusty sleigh bells and strung them on sticks around the house. But he made it. Burst in the door and there, sure enough, was a bottle of rotgut sitting on the table.

The old man jumped for the bottle but Sandy got it first. "Oh no you don't!" He put the flat bottle into his huge tunic pocket and buttoned it shut.

"What you do?" the old man asked.

"I'm going to take you back to town – along with this evidence. Six ounces is all I need, so there'll be plenty here. Get your coat, it's chilly out."

The old man reached for his coat which was hanging near the stove. Beside the stove was a box full of wood and as Sandy took his eyes off him for a second the old man picked up a piece of stove-wood and smashed it against the tunic pocket, breaking the bottle.

But Sandy was quick, too. He unbuttoned his tunic, took it off, grabbed a water glass from the table and squeezed the foul-smelling brew into it. He had just over the six ounces. I suppose you could say he got his man.

"The trouble is," Sandy told me, "now I can't get this damned stink out of my tunic. I've sent it to the cleaners but it's no good. What do they put in that stuff anyway?"

I got a letter back from the syndicate editor when I submitted this story, which I titled "Six Ounces of Evidence." He said that it was just an incident, not a story. To make a story it needed more conflict, possibly between the Mountie and his superior. Or perhaps I could bring a girl into it. I didn't know just where the girl would fit, there being no females on the force at the time, but I finally made this episode the key element in the Mountie getting a promotion and thereby being able to marry a girl. It didn't work. I liked it much better the first way.

Percy Ardley was an Englishman. He spoke with an English accent. He was cultured and refined and superior. I'm not sure that he was actually so superior come to think of it, as much as he made the rest of us blokes feel inferior. Especially in the eyes of our women. He made them discontented with their lot, for he had been everywhere, done everything and knew about art and music and the dance. The rest of us, having been born and raised in Saskatchewan, didn't know much about these things. Actually, I guess we *were* inferior.

Percy was nice about it though. He believed that it was part of his role in "the colonies" to elevate the natives. Civilize them. So he never hesitated to share his great fund of knowledge with us and to correct us when we made a gaff. This was particularly true when it came to tennis.

Tennis was our chief recreation in the spring, fall and summer. Over in the fair grounds about a quarter of a mile from our house there was an old tennis court, all overgrown with weeds. A group of us got together and fixed it up. We scraped it level, got a load of shale and spread it around, got a new net and repaired the fence. I dug out a picture of this the other day, and I must admit it didn't look much — grass growing up through the shale around the edges, weeds all around, patched fence. But I can never remember it looking like that when we lived in Wannego. It was our summer recreation centre.

On Saturday we'd pack a lunch and walk over to the court in the morning, me carrying Beryl on my shoulders. She'd sit on a blanket or toddle after grasshoppers or play with her pup, Puddles. About six other couples would come along, too. There were Danny and Yvonne Beltier and Rick Tapley who worked on the railway and Ruth, one of the waitresses from the hotel, and whichever Mountie happened not to be on duty and Mary Simms, who worked in the bank. Mary was always the girl-friend of the current Mountie. She was thirtyish and friendly and very easy to be with. Vincent Denis and his wife and the DeSantes also played. It was a nice, friendly little group.

We'd take turns playing in an easy relaxed manner, and those who weren't playing sat on the sidelines in the blazing sun and watched and talked and fooled around. Nice.

That is, it was nice until Percy showed up. To begin with, he told us that we weren't playing tennis at all.

"I know," I admitted, "but we're trying."

"No, I don't mean that, old boy. This game is properly called lawn tennis."

"On this court?"

"No, you see, there are two games – Tennis and Lawn Tennis. Tennis is much the older game. Sometimes it is called Royal Tennis or, in the U.S., Court Tennis. It is an indoor game. This that you are playing is properly called Lawn Tennis although it is often played on a clay court."

I knew right then we were going to have trouble.

Then he walked about our court digging little holes in it with his heels and shaking his head.

"Who is the president of your club?" he asked.

"Oh we don't have any president," Mary Simms told him. "We just play."

"Well, I suppose that accounts for the wretched condition of your court." We all looked at it then, as though seeing it for the first time, and it certainly did look wretched.

"It's okay," I quipped. "We play a wretched brand of tennis, donchaknow."

This got a slight snicker from the others but Percy just turned on me and gave me that English look. I think that was the last funny I attempted in his presence.

"No," Percy proclaimed. "We'll have to get to work and put this court in shape. That's the first thing."

So, instead of playing, we worked. Under the direction of Percy we took up all the tapes and scraped and raked the surface until we had all the chickweed, dandelions and grass out of it.

"Now we'll need new tapes," Percy told us. "Can't go putting those old tattered things down again."

But before we could raise money for new tapes we had to organize into a club. This we did, with proper parliamentary procedure under the direction of Percy. He wouldn't be president himself but he thought Danny Beltier should be because he was the only really permanent resident of the town amongst us all and, besides, through him we could get stuff wholesale. "You see the value of organization," Percy told us.

When we had all finished, the court did look better but it played a lot worse. Where we'd removed the weeds and grass was all soft now where once it had been hard. No matter how much we rolled it, we couldn't get it hard again.

There were other visual improvements, too. We had always played tennis in whatever we had – shorts, khaki pants, any old shirt with the sleeves rolled up. Didn't matter much. But the first day Percy appeared on the court carrying his two tennis racquets under his arm all that changed. He was a vision in white! Beautifully pressed white slacks, a white v-neck sweater, white tennis shoes and a choice white eyeshade. He looked like something right out of an *Illustrated London News* story on Wimbledon, a fine trim yacht among coal barges, a sleek thoroughbred among farm horses.

Besides this, Percy had a car and none of the rest of us did. It was a cream-coloured convertible, I remember, and he loved it dearly. He kept it polished and shined as he did his belt and shoes, even scraped the grasshopper remains from the front grille. He'd drive up to the court, wheel around, stop and, instead of opening the door and getting out like any decent person, he'd leap nimbly over the door and come smiling towards us.

"Here comes King Shit from Turd Island," Rick Tapley would whisper, but never loud enough for Ruthie to hear him.

For Percy was a great favourite with all the girls. He'd persuaded the club to go into debt for one of those round metal garden tables with big umbrella, "Excellent for afternoon tea . . ." and there they'd sit, Percy and the women.

We could hardly get any of them on the court any more. Afraid to muss up their nice white tennis ensembles. They much preferred to listen to Percy tell of his adventures in India, Australia and South Africa and other places where the sun never sets.

"This is no good," Rick complained. "That damned limey is buggering up the works. I'd rather be down at the pool room."

This was serious. We had barely enough tennis players as it was and to lose one to the poolroom would be disastrous. As a matter of fact, I wasn't getting any fun out of tennis any more, either.

I was a smash-bang sort of tennis player. My first serve was powerful and cut across the net like a bullet. That is unless it hit the net, which it did about nineteen times out of twenty. Then my second serve was a nice gentle little thing that came over soft and easy and could be killed by any real tennis player. Until Percy showed up we hadn't any real tennis players to kill it.

In doubles I was a demon at the net. I'd stand right up close when my partner was serving and catch half our opponents' returns, twisting my racquet cleverly so that the ball came straight down and was impossible to get. The first time I did this against Percy, he said, "Our point!"

"What do you mean, your point?"

"Your racquet was over on our side of the net."

"Huh?"

"You see, old boy, you must keep to your own side. It's against the rules to reach over."

"But I always do it this way!"

"Then you always do it improperly. If you'd just stand back about a foot, now, there'd be no danger of an illegal procedure."

"A what?"

"A foul, old boy."

I was getting it at home, too. "Do you really think you should play tennis in those old blue denims?" Aileen suggested.

"Why in hell not?"

"Well, you must admit they're not very elegant. And another thing . . ."

"Another thing?"

"Throwing your tennis racquet when you lose a point."

"What's wrong with that? I've always done that."

"Well, it's really not very sportsmanlike."

"What difference does that make? This isn't Wimbledon, you know."

She laughed gaily. "I rather think not."

My wife – my own wife – talking like a bloody Englishman – or Englishwoman. It was too much. "Oh for Christ sake!" I blurted out.

"Please," she said, "don't be so crude. I don't see why you must swear all the time."

It was then I knew we were in real trouble. More and more often, one or another of the men had an excuse for not coming out to play tennis. It wasn't just that the women often didn't want to play – preferring to sit in the shade and talk – or that Percy always beat the pants off us. Even when he wasn't playing you could feel his eyes on you and it put you off your game. My percentage of successful first serves dropped from 5 per cent to less than 1 per cent; my backhand which had always been a bit weak became hopeless. I was about to give up the game.

I wrote a story about the whole situation. A screamingly funny story, I thought, about an Englishman who had moved into a Saskatchewan small town and, to quote Rick Tapley, buggered up the works. It didn't sell, though; I suspect because it was written with too much emotion. Good humorous writing requires detachment. The writer must be far enough removed from the situation so that he can view it calmly in retrospect and not use words like "bastard" and "sonofabitch" in describing his people.

And then came the Tennis Club Ball.

This, too, was Percy's idea. He explained at one of our regular club meetings – we spent more time at meetings now than on the court – that the social proclivities of a club must not be overlooked. "Why," he said, "even in India, which is further from centres of culture and civilization than we now find ourselves, it is possible to maintain the amenities."

It was shortly after he made this statement that Rick Tapley began calling him Lord Percy, and the name stuck. We were surprised later to find that the people of the district with whom Percy had had dealings had been calling him that for months.

The ball was held in the hotel dining room, which Percy called the ballroom, and now that I think of it this was probably what caused all the trouble. Rick lived in a room in the hotel, as indeed did Lord Percy and Sandy McAdam. The ball was not restricted to members of the Tennis Club but tickets could be purchased by the general public for two dollars a couple. The high price, Percy explained, would keep out undesirable elements. It didn't work, though. All the same people came.

It's a funny thing about parties. I mean the way they develop. Sometimes everything goes along just fine with people drinking sensibly and everybody behaving themselves. At other times with the same people all hell will break loose. Maybe it has something to do with the ions in the air, or perhaps the little people become involved. Whatever the reason, where liquor is present you never know what will happen.

I remember such a catastrophe during the war when I was an officer aboard H.M.C.S. *Unicorn* in Saskatoon. *Unicorn* was not moored in the Saskatchewan River, although that body of water might have held a ship. No, she was moored at the corner of First Avenue and 24th Street and she was a converted garage.

It was the custom of the navy to call the training divisions "ships." The ratings, who had been recruited from the farms and towns of Saskatchewan, where the largest body of water most had seen was a slough, were obliged to say they were "going ashore" when they left the garage by a side entrance and "coming aboard" when they came back in.

What had once been the showroom had been converted into a wardroom where the officers drank and lounged about when they weren't working. Since we'd gone straight from the penury of the depression into the affluence of the navy, we weren't accustomed to having everything new and so the furniture of the wardrooms was made up of stuff the peacetime reserve officers had scrounged from here and there. It wasn't bad, but it wasn't opulent, either.

Also most of us weren't accustomed to drinking much, so when we got into the wardroom where all we had to do was call for drinks and the steward would come running with them, and then we didn't pay for them but just signed a chit – well, we sort of went a bit wild.

The first couple of commanding officers we had were local men who had been in the reserves for years and, like the rest of us, were products of the depression. Then they sent us a chap from Toronto by the name of Green who was, as they say in the navy, very pukka. He undertook to make real British sailors out of us, bring us up to scratch.

He was always urging us to refurnish the wardroom in the style befitting the navy. "This junk you have here . . ." he said with great contempt, "it looks like the lounge in the Elk's Lodge." But the wardroom committee demurred. Although the canteen fund was healthy, we couldn't get over our habit of not spending money. So despite his constant urgings we kept dragging our feet.

Then we had a wardroom dinner, complete with all the trimmings. That is, we began drinking well beforehand, drank heartily all through the meal and continued drinking afterwards. Green introduced us to a custom which he said was very Navy, although I've never heard of it since, called "Dogs of War." This was a simple little game in which the captain could call "dogs of war" on one of the junior officers and all the rest would leap on him and forcibly remove his trousers. Well, things went on in this motif of gay abandonment until somebody threw a cushion at somebody else and then everybody was throwing things.

It seems hard to credit, even now, but before we had finished we had completely demolished every piece of furniture in that room. Lamps were pitched out windows onto 24th Street, chairs were pulled apart, the dining room table broken up like matchwood, chesterfields torn asunder. Afterwards we refurnished the wardroom.

I tell this story to illustrate my point that where alcohol is involved anything can happen.

So it was with the Wannego Lawn Tennis Club Ball. All husbands had been warned by all wives that we'd better behave like gentlemen. And we did. There was a good turnout and the dancing was refined and nice and all went well. That is, during the dance all went well.

It was the custom in Saskatchewan then, and may still be for all I know, for people to drink in hotel rooms. I've consumed more liquor sitting on the edge of a bed or on the floor with my back propped up against a dresser in a room jammed with other drinkers than I've ever consumed in a proper tavern or lounge. So it was that we forgathered in Rick Tapley's room for this purpose, and along about midnight Rick said, "Let's get old Fancy Drawers Percy drunk."

This turned out to be more difficult than we thought. Not that Percy didn't drink. Percy would drink any given amount. But he never got even slightly drunk. He was one of those disgusting drinkers who become more steady the more they drink. They walk a little more carefully, talk a little more precisely, and don't swing from chandeliers.

So as Percy became more sedate and serious, we became more abandoned and carefree. At one point Rick and I were running through the dark, dingy corridors of the hotel, banging on the doors of travelling salesmen and shouting, "Take cover! The gophers are revolting!"

And then we'd pound each other on the back and laugh fit to kill. But no matter what we did we couldn't break through the reserve of Sir Percy. And so we gave up. He had us and we knew it. Then about two o'clock in the morning I said I guessed it was time to go home and Rick said, "I'll drive you."

"Go on, you haven't got a car."

"I'll borrow Lord Percy's."

"Hey . . . do you think you'd better?"

"Sure, we're all friends together . . . members of the same tennis . . . excuse me, *lawn* tennis . . . club. Come on . . . get Aileen and I'll drive you home."

So we went back to the room where Percy was beguiling the women with lies about his exploits in India and shh-ed at Aileen and Ruthie to come. Finally they came and, with a great deal of giggling and guffawing from Rick and me, we went down the stairs and out to the street where Percy's car was parked.

"Have you got a key?" I asked.

"This car doesn't have a key . . . just a switch. Besides, a policeman doesn't need to lock his car. Who's going to steal a policeman's car?"

Aileen said she didn't think we should do it and Ruthie agreed, but Rick and I just piled into the car.

It was a great joke, really, and we all laughed heartily at it. Rick fumbled with the switch and got the car going, turned on the lights, drove to the corner, and there right in front of the car was Percy. He'd got his tunic on and his big hat and he looked very stern. He had his big revolver in one hand. He held up the other and shouted, "Stop, in the name of the law."

Well this was the funniest thing we'd seen yet and we laughed much more heartily than before. In fact, we literally fell out of the car with laughing.

"You two are under arrest!" Percy shouted, and he was very red in the face.

"God, what an actor," I bellowed and held my sides.

"I'll take the women home. But you two stay here until I return," Percy said, and we laughed even harder.

So Percy drove Aileen and Ruthie home and when he got back Rick was climbing up the telephone pole in front of the hotel and singing "Shine On Harvest Moon." Percy drove up and got out his car. I snatched his big round hat off his head and threw it up to Rick who hung it on a peg. Then we both laughed so hard he nearly fell off the pole.

Things became pretty vague after that. The next thing I knew clearly was that Rick and I were in one of the cells in the town hall. My right arm was sore as though it had been twisted, and a very angry Englishman in a R.C.M.P. uniform was standing outside the cell saying things like car theft and resisting arrest and making a public nuisance. Before I toppled over on the hard bunk and went to sleep I remember thinking that this was a hell of a situation for a school-teacher to be in.

The next thing I remember was waking up with a enormous headache. Not sick to the stomach or anything – just this head that felt as though a tractor had run over it. And Ernest Stoneman was unlocking the cell door.

"Are you okay?" he asked. "Can you make it home?"

"Think so. What happened?"

"Nothing. Forget it."

"Oh my God . . . we took Ardley's car. We didn't steal it . . . just borrowed it . . ." Rick protested, feeling his way up from the hard bunk.

"I know. Damned fool thing to do with a guy like that. No sense of humour, these Englishmen. Take themselves too seriously."

I looked at Stoneman then and realized what a good guy he was. A good, tough, Saskatchewan guy. The kind you can trust. "Thanks," I said.

Not long after that Ardley was transferred out of the Wannego division and we resumed our weekend tennis.

It was nice. We'd go over when we felt like it and play as much as we wanted. I went back to throwing my racquet when I was mad and swearing and leaning over the net and doing all those things one doesn't do on a lawn tennis court. Nobody mentioned the club again. The president just kept forgetting to call meetings. We heard through Stoneman that Ardley had been sent to the Arctic. God help the Eskimos.

Our life in Wannego and my writing career changed drastically after we got our first radio. When we'd lived in the hotel we'd listened sporadically to the radio in the rotunda, but since moving to the wee house we'd been completely without one. Then for eleven dollars and sixty-five cents we got a little brown set from Mike Wasylchuck and plugged into the world.

Through KSL Denver and Salt Lake City we received the programs of the U.S. networks, and when the CBC built their big transmitter at Watrous we were able to learn what was going on in Canada, too. With a twist of the knob it brought comedy, drama, music, sporting events, actualities, news, soap operas, right into our living room.

But first I must tell you about Mike Wasylchuck because his story is so much a part of the sad, crazy, frustrating life on the plains during the depression.

Mike was in Grade 12 when I first came to Wannego and he was a good, solid student. He was also one of the best athletes in the school, a good mixer in his quiet way, and a darned nice guy. The kind of guy that they might have picked as a Rhodes Scholar if he'd ever made it to university. And he was ambitious, terribly so, a condition that surely should be made of sterner stuff than Mike.

Mike's great ambition when he was in school was to be a doctor. There was no doctor in Wannego and I think he had some idea that he would return to his home town when he finished interning and spend a happy life fetching babies, treating measles, cutting out appendices, and generally taking care of his friends and neighbours.

But Mike had about as much chance of doing this as a snowball has of lasting until July. His father worked as a railway section hand and – when he wasn't getting bumped by men with more seniority – barely managed to support his family of six. Rather than providing money to send Mike to university, he needed help from his son in order to feed the family. And of course when Mike graduated with high honours from our school there was no job at all for him. He was, in the language of those who were gainfully employed, a bum.

After trying for months to get a job in town, Mike tried Saskatoon and then Regina and then took the long freight ride to Vancouver. He returned from there, too, finally.

He hung around town doing odd jobs when he could find them. Worked at stooking and pitching bundles when there was any crop to stook or pitch, and gradually set up in business for himself selling on commission everything from encyclopaedias to crab-apple trees. If a company needed an agent, Mike was it. He became a life insurance agent and pestered the farmers and business men of the town, who gladly would have bought from him if they'd had any cash. He sold automatic can-openers from door to door, and drove around in a rickety buggy, trying to convince farmers whose caragana hedges were dying of thirst that the way to salvation was to diversify by planting fruit trees. He sold Christmas cards and Easter cards in season, and a variety of lawn ornaments although no grass was growing anywhere. He spent most of his time on these junkets washing windows and putting on screens for ladies who had no man about the house and who also had no money to pay him.

I really think that Mike would have made it, finally, if he hadn't had the misfortune to fall in love. For in those pre-pill days when a young man fell in love with a girl he didn't just move in with her or take her hitch-hiking or in some other way begin sleeping with her. If he were a sincere, decent young man like Mike he felt that before sexual intercourse came marriage. And marriage took money.

To make matters worse, Mike had fallen in love with a girl who was removed from him by religion, race and social position. She was Anglo-Saxon and he was Polish; she was United Church and he was Catholic; she was reasonably well off, he didn't have a dime. Her father had a very low opinion of all hunkies and Mike's father, alas, qualified as a hunky.

She had sat in front of Mike in class and in Grade 12 he became aware of her as a most marvellous person and desirable woman. I suppose this is one of the natural hazards of universal education.

At about the time we bought our radio from him – Mike had the agency for that, too – we saw him often. Ever since leaving school he'd made a habit of coming to our house to talk and borrow books and play with Beryl and have the kind of rapport that made living under the wretched conditions of the Thirties possible at all.

"You got married," he pleaded. "How did you do it?"

"Well, I had a job. Not much of a job, but a job."

"How did you manage to get to Normal School?"

"Well, we lived in Saskatoon so I didn't have to board out, and I managed to borrow a little money from my brother."

"Yeah . . . that's out for me."

"Besides," I continued, "I married a girl who was of the same religion as I, the same family background, the same upbringing and who, like me, was used to being poor. It all helped."

"You're not helping me much."

"Why don't you forget the girl?" I asked. "Now is no time for young people to be thinking of getting married."

"Keerist!" he exploded. "Listen to the man! You're only a few years older than I am. You know what I'm going through."

"There are plenty of other girls in town, some of whom, I understand, are ready and willing."

He looked at me keenly to make sure I really was kidding

and it's a good thing he understood that I was because he had about six inches in height on me and out-weighed me by twenty pounds. There was no solution to his problem that I could see. The odds were all against him. In this enlightened land of freedom, in this enlightened twentieth century, he was as badly restricted by tradition and financial condition as he'd have been if born in Verona in the sixteenth century.

"I think I'll go out and get drunk or something, or maybe rob a bank," he said disgustedly as he got up to leave.

I laughed merrily at this because I knew that Mike didn't drink. As for robbing a bank, this is what we all used to say in the Thirties when were flat broke. "I think I'll rob a bank." Banks represented the only place where there was money and we simply meant that we were so desperate for money that we would do anything. But the next time I saw Mike he was in a cell under the Opera House and he looked as though he'd been drunk for a week.

Ernest Stoneman had dropped around at the school. "I've got a friend of yours in the coop," he said. "You'd better come and talk to him. I can't seem to get to him at all."

"Who?"

"Young Wasylchuck."

"My God. What did he do?"

"Robbed a bank."

So I went down to see Mike in the jail where he sat dejected and alone.

Gradually I pieced his story together. It's a good chance that he never would have got into trouble if he hadn't met up with Harmless Harvey. His real name was Harmsworth, but who was going to call a kid that? Harmless had been in Grade 12 with Mike. In fact they'd been in the same grade all through school. They'd played baseball and hockey together and hung around some together, but had never been real close friends. Harmless was a thin, wiry character with a sharp face and he was wily, and devious, and scheming. He talked out of the side of his mouth and always gave the impression that he had something good going for him. His school work was the same. Never good. But somehow he managed to slither through.

After graduation he hung around the poolroom mostly and made a few bucks hustling the odd, bored traveller who might wander in from the hotel. Then he hit the road and nobody saw much of him. There were rumours that he'd been in a riot in Vancouver and also in Regina. He was the kind of guy who might be on the edge of a crowd of honest protesters and would likely throw the first rock.

As fate would have it, Mike met him when he, Mike, was at his lowest point of desperation. Harmless had somehow manoeuvred a bottle of mare's sweat, which was a name given to a particularly vile and powerful brand of home-brew that was much used in the district because it was cheap and quick. The fact that it made people crazy drunk and practically lifted the top off your head the next day was beside the point.

Mike and Harmless got into the bottle and began to tell each other of their problems. With both it was the same – lack of money. They managed to get another bottle and then another and by noon they were beyond recall. It was then that Harmless said, "I know how we can get all the money we need."

"How?"

"Rob a bank."

"Oh sure." Mike rolled back in the hay of the barn where they were drinking. Giggled insanely, then leaped to his feet, drew an imaginary gun from his pocket and bellowed "Stick 'em up!" This was so funny that he fell over again with laughter.

"No, no, you goofy bastard," Harmless protested, I mean it."

"Okay. You mean it. Let's rob two banks. One for you

and one for me." This amused him so much that he fell over again.

"You might have a good idea at that," Harmless said. He was much more used to alcohol than was Mike and he was thinking. "I know a town – not too far from here – where there are two banks. One right across the street from the other."

"Great idea," Mike said. "Where do we get a gun?"

Well, Harmless had thought of that, too. He had a thirty-thirty revolver that he'd found or stolen somewhere and all they needed was some shells. So they went to the hardware store and got some shells, borrowed a pick-up truck from a friend and started off along back roads for the town with two banks. Mike rode most of the way straddling the hood and shooting at magpies that flew low across the road.

They made one stop along the way where they went into a general store, bought a pair of ladies' stockings and asked for two paper bags.

"What are those for?" Mike asked drunkenly.

"You'll find out," Harmless said. He was beginning to sober up just a little.

They drove down the main street of the town with two banks and parked the car in a small lot behind the OK Economy store.

"Now," Harmless explained, "it's simple. It's just about closing time so there'll be hardly anybody in the bank. Pull one of these stockings over your head so nobody will know you and go into the bank on the north side of the street and get the money. Put it into the paper bag and walk out. I'll do the same at the other bank, and we'll meet here and high tail out of town."

"Okay, Harm," Mike said and shook his hand. Something was very wrong, he knew, but he wasn't one to back out of a deal.

So they pulled the stockings over their heads and walked around the corner to the banks. Mike did exactly as he'd been instructed. He walked into the bank, waved his gun, got the money in his paper bag and went back to the car. But the car was gone.

Harmless had got cold feet when he reached the front door of his bank. He saw some people in there and decided the whole project was too dangerous. He also suddenly remembered he had no gun. So he rushed back to the car and drove off towards Wannego with the idea of giving himself up to the Mounties and thus saving his hide.

So there was Mike with a paper bag full of money and no car. He took off his silk-stocking disguise and tried to start one of the other cars in the lot. But the owner came and said, "What the hell are you doing?" and Mike left.

He went out onto the street and, by now was beginning to feel the miseries of sobering up. His mind wouldn't click properly so he went into the Chinese cafe, set his bag of money on the floor beside him, ordered a cup of coffee and drank it. Then he went out on the street again and tried to hitch a ride out of town.

A car stopped for him all right. But it was the Mountie's car. And so Mike was caught with the goods.

When he was brought to trial practically everybody in town appeared as character witnesses, and Mike got off with a year's suspended sentence. He went back to his many selling dodges and managed to hold on until the war started in 1939. Then of course young men like Mike were much in demand. He joined the airforce as soon as they would take him, and wore his shiny new uniform back to town with pride. Everybody was glad to see him. From being a bum he'd become a hero.

I'd like to be able to report that he rose in the ranks to become an officer and married his love and lived happily ever afterwards. The sad truth, however, is that he was killed in a training accident in Prince Albert when the DeHaviland Moth he was flying crashed into the bush and burned.

I kept the radio for long, long time, even after the war, and often when I'd turn it on I'd think of Mike. I would also remember how much radio had meant to us during those last years of the thirties.

Radio drama was at its peak – and such plays as the spooky thrillers by Arch Obler have never been surpassed for suspense and scariness. We'd turn out all the lights and listen and sometimes we had to turn them back on because we couldn't stand it. But the best of them all was *Mercury Theatre* with the boy wonder, Orson Welles, still in his twenties but with a personality so powerful it came right across the air waves. And one night we listened while he scared the people of New York out into the streets with his adaptation of H. G. Wells' *War of the Worlds*.

There was a Canadian drama series on then, too, called *The Canadian Theatre of the Air*, on which each week was a half-hour radio drama. This became my target. I began writing for radio. It was new, it was different and, most important, it seemed best suited to my temperament and approach to writing.

So I became a radio playwright. The idea of hearing words written by me spoken by Austin Willis or Jane Mallett became an obsession. I would have a group of friends in, I figured, and then at just the right moment casually turn on the radio and listen to my play. Then the credits. Then the exclamations of surprise and admiration from those same friends who had kidded me about my literary endeavours.

My first play was titled *Mountain Madcap*, and it featured a university student who had taken a job in the salad kitchen at Jasper Park Lodge (Aileen's sister Wilma had done this) and who met on the golf course a rather carelessly dressed young man whom she took to be one of the waiters. He in turn mistook her for a wealthy heiress and so we had a nice bit of mistaken identity which, as anybody knows, is the basis of most comedy.

Theatre Of The Mind

I was elated by the ease with which the scenes fell into place and with the witty dialogue I was able to put into the mouths of my principal characters. I felt great. I felt inspired. At last I had found my true *métier* in the literary world. I finished the play in a glow of enthusiasm, Aileen typed it up nice, and we sent it in to the CBC and waited.

In a surprisingly short time I received a letter from Mr. Edgar Stone, who stated that all the material for this show was cleared through his office before going to the sponsor for final consideration. He said he'd need two more copies of the script and three copies of a synopsis of the play, which would be "full enough to do your story justice without being cumbersome."

Well, this was a hell of a lot better than a rejection slip and so we got busy and typed up all the things he'd asked for and had them in the next mail. By this time the postmaster was excited about this as we were, although we'd sworn him to secrecy – just in case.

This time nothing happened at all. No letters, no phone calls, no wires. Nothing. *Mountain Madcap*, I suspect, is still sitting at the bottom of a dusty pile of scripts somewhere, about which a harried producer is saying he must do something soon.

One other thing happened in connection with that first radio that, in retrospect, still seems tragic to me no matter how hard I try to make it seem funny. We didn't win a car.

Since the radio was new to us and we were so isolated, we listened to everything. One of our favourite programs came on at one o'clock in the afternoon and lasted for fifteen minutes, just giving me time to hear it and still get to school. It was a soap opera, it was called *Big Sister*, and it was wonderful.

The word soap opera later became synonymous with corn and bathos, but when they were young and all the good plots hadn't been used up they were good. Big Sister became a real character to us. She was very modern, always protesting, always fighting the forces of corruption and graft and evil, which in those days meant big business. This was before big business began its public relations campaigns for respectability and bosses were still greedy monsters. Politicians were grafters and policemen were not above taking a bribe. Into this mess waded *Big Sister*, eyes flashing – I suppose, although we couldn't see them – stern of voice, radiating truth and honour and justice. I'm sure that every afternoon I went to school a better man because of *Big Sister*.

And on the show they took to giving things away, much as they are doing now, as a matter of fact. At first it was little cameos with *Big Sister's* face on them, real Sheffield steel carving knives with cocabola wood handles, and a set of five silver teaspoons with a Dionne quintuplet on each handle. We got all these things.

Then one day they announced that they were giving away to the lucky winner a brand new car and a year's supply of gasoline. All you had to do was state in fifteen words or less why you liked Cleanso Soap. Well, being writers we were sure we could write the slogan they were looking for. We wrote dozens and sent them in with box tops. We had enough soap to last us until Beryl would be a grandmother.

Strange how one can get caught up in a thing like that. We so desperately wanted to win that car. In the summer we'd drive to Banff, or Hollywood maybe. See new places, experience new things. Neither Aileen nor I had ever been out of Saskatchewan except for short camping trips when we were kids, and we couldn't remember much about that.

And because we so desperately wanted the car we actually came to believe we were going to get it. We'd lie in bed at night thinking up new and better slogans and talking of the things we'd do during the next summer holidays. "A writer," I explained, "has to go places and do things. I need new material."

There was to be a winner each day for a week. Five new cars. Surely one of them would be ours. Each day's winner was announced at the conclusion of the program, and for four days I listened and got up sadly and walked over to the school, thinking the next day would be our turn. Then on Friday the big announcement came.

"Today's car," the smooth voice on the radio purred, "goes away out to Saskatchewan . . ." We held our breath. It was actually going to happen. I knew as surely as I had ever known anything in my life that the name he would say would be mine. But it wasn't. It was some woman in Elfros or a place like that. Not even a writer, probably. Just a farm wife. We had no car.

So I wrote a short story about a couple who had won a car in just such a contest and had taken a trip in it, and how it had completely ruined their lives. All this affluence, you see, had changed their values and made greedy, aggressive people of them. It was supposed to be a comedy, but I don't think it was very funny. It didn't sell.

After that it was even harder to get myself up for the daily writing stint. Many a morning when the alarm would go off at five I'd lie there and think, "What the hell? This isn't getting you anywhere. Who are you kidding, anyway? You're never going to make it. Why don't you quit?"

But I'd get up. A desperate man doesn't quit. Stumbling across the desert towards water a man doesn't quit. He'll crawl on his belly and claw the sand until he dies. Well, I was stumbling all right, stumbling badly. But I hadn't fallen on my belly yet. I didn't quit for the same reason that the man on the desert doesn't quit. Quitting meant death, and I figured I was too young to die.

Two things I remember about 1937. One, it was the year it didn't rain. At least, not in our part of the province. Not a drop. And two, it was the year I finally got flaming mad.

All of us like to believe that we are masters of our own fates, architects of our own lives, and to a large extent we are. But chance, plain ordinary accident, has more to do with shaping our lives than most of us like to admit. For instance, if a dear old lady hadn't died in Victoria – or somewhere on the West Coast – in the summer of 1937, there's a strong likelihood that I'd still be in the teaching game today.

During that hot, windy spring Harry King and I were working like dogs trying to get the senior students through their final examinations. There was no kidding about these exams. They were set by the Department of Education and marked in Regina, and we had absolutely no control over the results.

Each student wrote under the strictest supervision. The examination envelopes were never opened until the moment of truth – just before the writing time – and each completed paper was immediately stuffed into a special envelope and sealed and identified only by number. There were affidavits to sign and legal stuff like that to be gone through, and it was all very tense and exciting.

This has been described by modern education experts as being all bad. But I wonder if it was. There was an excitement about examination time, a fresh flowing of adrenalin, a hard thumping of the heart. It was the moment of challenge. The climax to the year's work. A student either made it or he didn't. Nobody could help him; nobody could hinder. He was strictly on his own. Like a trained boxer, he faced his opponent. Seconds out of the ring. The gong goes. It was a form of natural selection.

Besides, the student could make up for a lot at exam time. If he'd been swinging the lead all year he could come on strong at the end by a concentrated rush of work. No matter how much he'd antagonized a teacher during the term, that teacher couldn't do for him in the end. That teacher had nothing to do with the results.

This has been criticized as not being the "true meaning of education." Maybe not, maybe so. Perhaps it's good to learn that a strong effort at the right time will see you through. Isn't this what the salesman does in making a sale, or a politician in getting elected, or a tycoon in swinging a merger, or a writer in finishing a book, or an actor in getting ready for a part? That's the way it's done and maybe it's good to learn that in high school.

After all, what else do we learn in high school that stays with us? Students study French for four years, but how many can speak French at the end? Mathematics, unless one is going to specialize in the subject, is forgotten in months. We learn more about history from a few good books than we ever do from teachers.

Anyway, there was a feeling of excitement in the air. We were reviewing the English and History courses extensively and most of the kids were working hard. It was during this that Harry King casually said to me at recess, "I hear they're looking for a principal for the Birchley school. Why don't you go after it?"

"Do you think I'd have a chance?"

"Well, I taught there before I came here. I know most of the men on the board. My recommendation might help."

"Thanks. But I don't have a university degree."

"Neither do I. As long as you're working at it, it's okay."

I thought about this. A principal's job might pay as much as a thousand dollars a year. Wow!

"But what about your writing career?" Aileen asked when I told her.

"Some career. One lousy sale for five bucks."

"But you've come close."

"Close doesn't buy groceries. Besides, I wouldn't have to quit writing."

"You'd have to start the university courses again."

"I know, but I can do that, too."

We both knew this was impossible. "I just might be able to get this job," I said. "After all, it's a chance that may not come again for a long time. You know . . . 'take the current as it serves. . . .' "

So Harry and I went down to Birchley on the morning train. He hadn't overstated the case. He was popular there. Many people told him he was the best principal they'd ever had.

"But remember," Harry warned me, "it will be up to you to sell the board. I can run a little interference for you but you'll have to carry the ball yourself." Harry liked such similes.

I carried the ball, all right. In fact I was inspired. I convinced that group of farmers and businessmen that their school would be a better place with me at its head. And they hired me. We signed the contract then and there.

When we got back to Wannego on the evening train, Aileen wasn't as delighted as she might have been. I think she realized that my high spirits were a bit forced. That I was trying to make this cop-out seem like the best move for all concerned. I talked too loudly and confidently, I guess. Anyway, she was troubled.

When the exams were all over and the holidays finally came, I appeared at the University of Saskatchewan and enrolled in a psychology class, along with my friend Craig Mooney who was also married and had one child and was teaching in another part of the province and trying to sell stories to magazines. I paid five dollars down on my fee.

Aileen and Beryl and I moved once again into the second floor of her folks' house on Temperance Street and I began the long, hot walks up to the university each morning to sit in a hot, stuffy room and watch the big bluebottles buzzing around the window and try to absorb some psychology. As a starter, the professor asked us to write an account of our lives up to that moment, explaining how we came to be in his class.

The second day when I got home Aileen said, without looking at me, "There's a letter for you. It's from the Department of Education."

I opened it and it was from the Deputy Minister of Education, a man named McEachney, and it said that they were in receipt of a copy of the contract signed by me and the school board at Birchley, and that they regretted to inform me that, due to a new regulation, I could not fill this position as principal of a four-room continuation school because I didn't have a university degree. Or words to that effect. He also added a strange paragraph to say that they would wait one week for word from me before making the final decision.

I took this to mean that if I could swing enough influence they might make an exception in my case. After all, half the principals in the province didn't have university degrees.

"Do you know anybody in the Department?" Mooney asked me.

"I think I know Mr. Estey."

"The Minister of Education! What do you mean you *think* you know him?"

"He lived two doors from us when I was a kid. I used to play with his son."

"Well, that's your answer. Get all your inspectors' reports and recommendations and so on and go and see him. He just lives a few blocks from you over on Saskatchewan Crescent."

Great. I was saved. I phoned the Honourable Mr. Estey.

Yes, he remembered me, and yes, he'd be glad to see me. That evening would be fine.

So that fine July evening with the crickets singing in the grass I walked over to Mr. Estey's house where it sat on the bank of the Saskatchewan River. I felt pretty confident, I remember. The lights from the Twenty-fifth Street bridge were reflected in the river and the wind was gently rustling the leaves of the aspen and white birch. I went through the front gate of his yard, up the walk onto the big veranda, and knocked on the door. No answer. I knocked again. Still no answer. Finally a woman came to the door, I don't know who.

"Is Mr. Estey in?" I asked.

"No. He left just a few minutes ago."

"Oh. Will he be back later tonight?"

"No. He's gone to Victoria. [I think it was Victoria.] You see he just received a telegram that his mother died and he barely had time to catch the train."

"Oh. I'm sorry to hear it. When do you think he will be back?"

"Not for several weeks, I'm afraid."

And that was that. Within a week I had another letter from McEachney stating that, since there had been no word from me, they would have to invoke the regulations and deny me permission to be principal. So I wrote to Birchley and learned that McEachney had been in touch with them, too. They said they were sorry, and suggested that, since they'd hired a university graduate with no experience as vice-principal, he and I could change jobs. Perhaps, they suggested, I'd be willing to sort of help him with the discipline – considering that he had no experience and all.

But I wanted no part of that. If I was going to remain a vice-principal, I'd do it in Wannego where I had friends. I phoned Jim Walters, the chairman of the board. No, they hadn't got around to hiring a new teacher yet. Yes, I could have my job back if I wanted it. No, they couldn't give me a raise in salary.

We hadn't moved our furniture out of the little house yet, and so nothing was changed there. Nothing was changed anywhere except that now I was flaming mad.

Suddenly the whole rotten mess of the depression and the teaching conditions came sharply into focus. Slum schools, impoverished teachers, wretched living conditions, stupid, arrogant school boards, the putrid position of the school-teacher in the community. The whole festering bag.

I'd known all this before, of course, but this last slap in the face from a system I'd served faithfully for six years was too much. I would write an article and expose to the rest of Canada the wrongs being perpetrated against teachers and children – nay, to the whole world.

To hell with school teaching, anyway. I'd have nothing more to do with it ever. I went to the registrar of the university and retrieved my five bucks. I told the psychology prof that, instead of writing an essay explaining how I came to be in his class, I'd write an article to explain why I wasn't. He looked at me as though I were nuts. I broached the idea to my friend Mooney, and he agreed to collaborate. Together we would slay the dragon of indifference and neglect.

So we went at it. In the office of the Saskatchewan Teachers' Federation we found an ally in the executive-secretary, Jack Sturdy. He had a filing cabinet stuffed with letters from teachers. Letters that told of teaching in cold, drafty schools and living in cold, drafty farm houses. Of receiving no pay whatsoever and living on relief. Of being fired for rejecting the son of the chairman of the school board. Of one drinking cup for a room of forty kids, and on and on and on. Each letter signed, each authenticated.

"Go ahead," Jack Sturdy said. "Use what you need. It's time somebody paid some attention."

I'm sure he never really believed the article would be published.

When we began to write that article I discovered an important truth. The best thing for a writer is some good, honest rage. Get mad. See red. Be indignant, but try to keep it under control. The material we had was so loaded, so true and so damning that it required no embellishment from us. A straightforward presentation of the facts would do the trick.

While we were about it, we took a poke at the Department of Education, the local school board system, which we described as archaic and vicious, the attitude of parents, the provincial Normal School, which was a farce, and even the school inspectors, who had considerable control through their reports over our jobs.

We signed a couple of fictitious names to the article and sent it with a letter to Mr. Napier Moore, editor of *Maclean's* magazine. We explained in the letter that we were principal and vice-principal respectively of four-room schools, and that much of our material was from the Teachers' Federation files.

I was so accustomed to sending manuscripts in the mail and never hearing about them again that I forgot about this one. Then one hot August day when I was sitting on the front veranda of the Temperance Street house reading a magazine, the mailman came up the walk and handed me a letter. It was from *Maclean's.*

I got that same old letter jitters that had afflicted me ever since I'd begun trying to sell writing. Here was a letter. Sealed. Inside it was a message. It might be good or it might be bad. The tenor of that message meant so much to me that again I couldn't open the letter. I bounced it up and down on the fingers of one hand, looking at it. At least I'd prolong the moment of hope.

The screen door banged behind me and Aileen asked, "Who's the letter from?"

"*Maclean's.*"

"No! What does it say?"

"I haven't opened it yet. Kind of heavy. Not just a rejection slip. Wonder what it says."

"Why not open it and see?"

"Uh . . . you open it." I handed the letter to her and she ripped it open, read it, gasped and handed it to me.

The letter was signed by H. Napier Moore himself. I noticed that first. And it said in a matter-of-fact way that they liked our article and would publish it if we'd agree to use our own names. Just like that.

It's always struck me as somehow wrong that an editor could take this thing so calmly. I mean, such an important message should surely call for a "congratulations" or a "nice going" even. But there was nothing like this. Just a nice, formal business letter.

Well, they might be calm but I wasn't. I leaped about six feet in the air, bussed my wife soundly, and dashed in to phone Mooney. He agreed it would be all right for them to use our real names and we got a letter off to H. Napier Moore saying so. I felt so good I couldn't keep still. Kept giving little jumps in the air and taking little sprints as I walked along the street. An article in Canada's best read and most influential magazine!

And then the reaction set in. All those things we had said. This wasn't just a shot in the dark any more. This would be read by the principal of the Normal School and the inspectors and school board members. Maybe we should have been a little more cautious there. The printed word is so official and final.

In September, when we'd already gone to Wannego, I received a wire from Moore saying the article was scheduled for October and did we want to make any changes? I wired back to let it go as written, and in due course the article appeared. There it was – right near the front of the book. An illustration of a bleak little schoolhouse in the midst of a dust storm and the title "School Drought." Beneath this in big letters – By CRAIG M. MOONEY AND J. M.

BRAITHWAITE. It was the first time I'd seen my name in print and it looked mighty good. It was, incidentally, the last time I ever used that by-line.

I sat with the open magazine in my hand and thought of all the great names I'd seen there – Stephen Leacock, Leslie MacFarlane, George Drew, Gratton O'Leary, Robert Service, Ralph Connor. And there was mine, right along with them. Hot dog! It's the greatest thrill in the world, one I've never gotten over.

Mooney and I waited with heads bowed for the great weight of the educational establishment to crush us to death. Other teachers looked at us askance. "Aren't you afraid you'll lose your certificates?" they whispered.

With a confidence that was only partly put on, we answered, "So what? Of what use is a certificate that enables you to earn a pittance for a full year's work and dooms you to second class citizenship?" Besides, we said, this is a free country. Surely it's still possible to speak out against wrong wherever you find it. Surely there is some justice in the land.

It is difficult in these times of protest and demands being made by all classes of society to realize that we were so timid during the Thirties. But it must be remembered that people were jailed and deported for holding radical views. That men were killed during the Regina riots, and the attitude towards all who protested was a stern one. As Prime Minister R. B. Bennett had said earlier in the decade, "We ask every true Canadian to put the iron heel of ruthlessness against a thing of this sort."

As it turned out, nothing was done to hurt us. The principal of the Saskatoon Normal School wrote an indignant letter challenging us to a public debate. Knowing something of his speaking ability, we politely declined and suggested that he write an article of his own. The Honourable J. W. Estey wrote an article, in rebuttal, which said a lot of things to refute the things we'd said. *Maclean's* ran it in one

You've Got To Get Flaming Mad

of the back pages. The inspectors were quite distant when they called and gave us indifferent reports, but this didn't matter much as few school boards even read these reports anyway, preferring to go by their own estimates of the teacher's character and ability.

I've no idea what effect this article had on the speed of educational reform in Saskatchewan, but I know it had a tremendous effect on me. It came at a critical point in my life when I was deciding whether to be a teacher or a writer, and it was just enough weight to tip the scales. If Mr. Estey's mother – or whatever relative it was – hadn't died and taken him out of town, I probably would have gone to Birchley as principal and surely never would have helped write that article.

It doesn't take much encouragement to keep a neophyte writer at his task, but it takes some. With my half of the fee ($37.50) I bought a better used typewriter and went back to writing. I besieged *Maclean's* with ideas for articles, but they all turned out to be articles they already had in the works or for some reason or other weren't interested in. It's possible for a beginning writer a couple of thousand miles away from editors to score once or twice, but it's difficult to keep it up. Most ideas, I subsequently learned, come from the editors and are assigned to writers on the spot.

So I went back to writing stories and plays and learning the craft. The whole thing of becoming a principal and going on with the university courses had been a mistake. McEachney hadn't really done me dirt; he'd done me a favour. He had, in fact, rescued me. It was an omen, I was sure. Once again my guardian angel had taken a hand and gently steered me along the right and proper path.

My writing was improving, too. I could see that. My short stories had more form and meaning. My radio plays were better dramatically. Now and then I managed to sell one to the CBC and pick up a few dollars. My apprenticeship was ending, but I was still a thousand miles from the markets and saw no way of getting there.

Then I got a really big break. Hitler attacked Poland, England declared war, Canada followed suit, and everything changed. Money that had been so tight for ten years suddenly became plentiful. Men who were superfluous for as long as many could remember suddenly were in great demand. Nothing was too good for them. They were given pay, clothing, housing, travel vouchers, shiny uniforms, and most of all self-respect. They were needed. They had some purpose in life. To defeat the forces of evil, that was their purpose.

You can't beat a war for stirring a country up, for bringing it out of the doldrums of lethargy, for starting the adrenalin flowing, the flags waving, the speeches spouting. Rich and poor were all one now. There were no more bums. Just valiant Canadians marching off to do their duty. Excitement was in the air, and glamour. We all had something to pull for and something to hate. We were united, to quote Mackenzie King again, "in a common cause."

Make no mistake about it, many of my generation of Saskatchewanites were saved by the war. Boys I'd known at school who were brilliant and never had a chance to prove it joined the army or the air force or the navy and gained rank the way a healthy steer gains weight. Soon they were lieutenants, flying officers, colonels. They had a chance to prove their worth. The war set them on a ladder of success and they never stopped climbing.

When I was discharged from the navy in the fall of 1945 I found myself – four years older and with two more kids – in Toronto, and I decided I would never leave. I would stay and make my living as a free-lance writer.

Everything that had been so unnatural, impossible in fact, on the prairies now became natural and relatively easy. For I was in the land of the editors, producers and publishers. The end of the war brought a spectacular increase in communications. Everybody, it seemed, wanted something written and there were few writers around to do the job. At last I was in the right place at the right time. I said I was a writer and people believed me. They assigned me things to write and, because of the time I'd put in at Wannego learning the craft, I was able to do a passable job.

So I became a full-time writer – aggressive, busy and content. Ontario became my home, and Ontario is as unlike Saskatchewan as it is possible to be. The cold, dust storms, poverty and indifference of the prairies became a memory. At first a bitter memory, but as time passed a fond memory. For the great compensating factor of the plains is the people. Like the climate they are harsh at times, gentle at others, but never dull.